Hope

Happens

clearwater crossing

Hope Happens

laura peyton roberts

BANTAM BOOKS
NEW YORK • TORONTO • LONDON • SYDNEY • AUCKLAND

RL 5.8, age 12 and up
HOPE HAPPENS
A Bantam Book / January 2000

ISBN 0-553-49297-7

For Renee,
who knows it does

Blessed are those who have not seen and yet have believed.

John 20:29

One

This is just great, Jenna Conrad thought, feeling completely foolish.

She pushed her books around on the table in front of her, trying to look busy and hoping no one was watching. She was practically the only student in the library that noon—probably only two or three other people had even noticed her—but her cheeks still burned with the shame of being so pathetic. Bending her head over an open text, she hid behind the curtain of her long brown hair.

This is stupid.

Who studied during lunchtime on the Tuesday after a three-day weekend? She didn't even have anything to work on. All the normal people were in the cafeteria, eating. Jenna imagined the noise level in the big, echoing room being even greater that day than usual as everyone discussed what they'd done on Presidents' Day and shared the details of their Sunday-night Valentine's Day dates. Normally she loved the bustle of the first day back at school after a holiday. She looked forward to hearing her friends' stories and telling her own, then going over the best parts a second time with her boyfriend, Peter Altmann.

Not this time. The last thing she wanted to talk about was her own, disastrous Valentine's Day date, and if she had to hear about someone else's perfect evening, she would almost certainly cry. As far as talking the details over with Peter went . . .

Peter's the last person I want to see.

She still couldn't close her eyes without immediately envisioning that horrible scene in Le Papillon: Peter confessing that he'd kissed Melanie Andrews, Jenna drawing all eyes by knocking over her water glass. He'd sworn it meant nothing, that he wished it had never happened. He'd apologized over and over. But nothing could take away the sting of that betrayal. Jenna had always suspected him of having a crush on Melanie—and he had finally given her proof. The busboy had hurried over to change their dripping tablecloth, resetting the table as if nothing had happened, but he needn't have bothered as far as Jenna was concerned. The evening had already been ruined.

Somehow she had choked out an acceptance to Peter's apology. She had even managed to eat her fancy French dinner. She had changed the subject, she had smiled and pretended to enjoy dessert—she had done whatever it took to get through the meal with a minimum of extra drama. But when Peter had finally dropped her off at her door, she hadn't kissed him good-night. And she'd barely spoken to him since.

"What should we do tomorrow?" he'd asked, lingering at her front door.

"Tomorrow? I'm busy," she'd blurted out.

"Doing what?"

"I promised Sarah I'd do something with her. She's been bugging me for weeks, so I finally said yes."

"Oh," he'd replied, disappointed. "I'd kind of assumed we'd do something together."

"Sorry," she'd said, feeling anything but. She had shut the door without clarifying that she'd promised to do something with Sarah the *following* weekend, not that one.

Things had only gotten worse when her older sister Caitlin had arrived home from her date with Peter's brother, David. By then Jenna had temporarily stopped crying, but she was still lying awake in the girls' third-floor bedroom, waiting to pour out her troubles to a sympathetic listener. Normally shy Caitlin had been so elated about her big first date with David, however, that she was the one who had done all the talking, raving about the restaurant, the dinner, the movie—even the iced tea. She'd obviously had such a good time that Jenna couldn't bring herself to admit what a heartbreaking experience her own evening had been. Instead she had claimed it was fine.

3

And having said nothing then, when her disappointment was freshest, Jenna found herself even less inclined to own up the next day. At breakfast, every member of her family had been making plans to enjoy the Monday holiday. Caitlin was going bowling with David, Maggie and Allison were both headed off to see friends, and Mr. and Mrs. Conrad were going furniture shopping. Only Sarah and Jenna couldn't say what they'd be doing.

"You girls are welcome to come shopping with us," Mr. Conrad had said. "We're going to look at new sofas for the den."

"Yippee." Sarah hadn't bothered to disguise her lack of interest in that idea. "I think I'll walk to Value-Mart and buy a new book."

"I'm going to practice my guitar," Jenna had said quickly. "I haven't played in a long time."

But long before Sarah had returned from the store, Jenna had put the guitar away, too upset even to sing. She was lying on her back, staring at the ceiling, when Sarah stuck her head into the bedroom.

"I thought you were going to practice," Sarah had said, looking around for the guitar.

"I don't feel like it," Jenna had replied without moving.

Sarah had apparently taken her sister's lack of activity for some sort of invitation. "Really? Do you want to play Monopoly?" she'd asked, walking over to sit on Caitlin's bed.

"What?" Jenna had said irritably, casting her sister a disbelieving look.

Sarah was leaning forward on the bed, her straight, shoulder-length blond hair swinging toward her sharply pointed chin. Her wide blue eyes met Jenna's, full of misplaced hope. "Monopoly?"

"No, I don't want to play Monopoly! I just want to be left alone."

"You don't have to yell," Sarah had told her, offended.

"I don't even know why you're in here. I told you we'd do something *next* weekend. Can't you give a person some peace?"

Sarah had leapt to her feet. "Fine! Have all the peace you want," she'd said, slamming the door behind her.

Jenna had considered going downstairs to make up, but in the end she had stayed where she was. She'd had enough on her mind already without pretending she wanted to play Monopoly. Besides, the whole fight had been Sarah's fault.

Now, though, hiding behind her hair in the CCHS library, the memory of their argument only added to Jenna's sense of how alone she was.

I could end this right now, she thought. *I could get over myself, go to the cafeteria, and have lunch with Peter.*

There was nothing to stop her. Since she'd claimed to accept his apology, he didn't even know she was still mad at him. In fact, he was probably wondering where she was at that very minute.

Let him wonder, she thought, her head sinking a little lower.

She felt like an idiot hiding from Peter when she still loved him so much, but she didn't know what else to do. How could he have kissed someone else in the first place, let alone kept it a secret all those months? He had hurt her so unbelievably, she just didn't think she could look him in the face.

And she wasn't in any hurry to see Melanie again, either.

"I'll try to call you tonight," Miguel del Rios said, stopping his car at the curb beside the Rosenthals' condominium building. "If I don't get home too late."

Leah reached reluctantly for the side door handle. "I wish you didn't have to go to work."

"I know," he said, a hint of impatience crackling in his brown eyes. "You *always* wish I didn't have to, but I always do."

"It's just that you work so many days! Why can't Sabrina give you more time off?"

"I don't *want* more time off. If I'm ever going to get my family a decent apartment, I need to make as much money as I can."

Leah bit back all the tart responses that immediately came to mind. Ever since she and Miguel had decided not to get married, it seemed like all he thought about was moving his family out of public housing and into a regular three-bedroom apartment. The fact that his mother, his younger sister, and he had been forced to take public assistance after the early and unexpected death of Mr. del Rios had been a thorn in Miguel's side ever since Leah had met him, but now that his mother's kidney transplant had allowed her to return to regular work and Miguel had a part-time job painting office buildings, he was practically obsessed.

"You must have nearly enough money to move by now." Leah knew his family needed two months' rent and a security deposit, but they'd been working and saving for a couple of months. "Can't you lighten up a little?"

"It isn't just about moving, Leah. You have to keep paying the rent once you get there."

"Whatever you say." By now she knew there was no point arguing when he got into one of his stubborn moods—no matter how right she was. Leaning across the gearshift, she brought her lips to his.

"Don't forget to call," she whispered.

And as she watched his old car drive away, she had to admit it wasn't really the hours that were bothering her anyway.

It was the person he was spending them with.

Miguel's boss, Mr. Ambrosi, was an old friend of the del Rios family, which was how Miguel had gotten his job. The problem was that Mr. Ambrosi wasn't the one supervising Miguel's services—his eighteen-year-old daughter, Sabrina, did that.

Sabrina Ambrosi, Leah thought with a shudder, walking into her lobby. Even the name sounded dangerous. And if Sabrina had to be on every job site, did she have to be absolutely gorgeous too? Leah knew her own looks were nothing to be ashamed of—she'd recently made the finals of a national modeling contest. But Sabrina had this raven-haired, violet-eyed, young-Liz-Taylor thing going that made Leah absolutely crazy. Not that she was *insecure*. But security had limits.

I'm not going to think about Sabrina, she decided, using the smallest key on her ring to open the Rosenthals' mailbox.

The box was stuffed with mail, most of it junk. Flipping quickly through the letters, bills, and flyers, Leah arrived at an item that made her heart start racing.

"Stanford!" she whispered, staring down at the envelope she'd been waiting for all her life.

But was it a yes or a no?

The contents felt like a single sheet of paper. Leah had been told that college acceptances were thin— but were they *this* thin? Her hands shook as she ripped the envelope open.

"Yes!" she shouted triumphantly, her voice echoing in the empty lobby. "Yes, I'm in!"

The thrill lasted only a few seconds, though, before the doubts rushed into her mind.

And what now? Would she go? And if she did, what would happen between her and Miguel? Or between Miguel and Sabrina, for that matter?

Leah sucked in a deep breath. *Of course I'll go. I'd be crazy not to.*

When she and Miguel had decided to call off their engagement, she had made it clear that she'd attend Stanford if she was lucky enough to get in. And it looked like she was in . . .

"I have to tell Mom and Dad!" she exclaimed, running for the stairs.

"I'm home!" Nicole Brewster shouted, slamming her front door.

Normally she didn't make that type of announcement—it was only a blatant invitation for someone to run out and force her to vacuum or dust or waste her time with something equally boring—but that Tuesday she felt too good to slink up to her room the way she usually did. She had just quit her job at Wienerageous, the obnoxious fast-food dive she'd been working at for the past few weeks, and she was so happy she was practically floating.

"Did you remember to turn in your uniform?" her mother asked, walking out from the kitchen.

"Are you kidding?" As if getting rid of that polyester affront to fashion hadn't been the top thing on her list. "No," Nicole said sarcastically. "I thought I'd save it for the prom."

Mrs. Brewster raised a warning eyebrow, then went ahead and smiled. "It wasn't something *I* would have wanted to wear," she admitted.

"Oh, I would have *loved* to see that!" Her mother always dressed as if she were expecting a camera crew any minute, even when her real plans only involved doing the laundry between soap operas. "What are we having for dinner?"

"Spaghetti. And it's going to be a while, so you might as well get busy on your homework."

"Okay. Sure will," Nicole promised, bounding up the stairs to her room. *Right after I call Courtney.*

It had been so long since she'd been able just to call and gossip with her best friend. First Courtney had been mad at her; then Nicole had been tied up with her secret job at Wienerageous nearly every afternoon. Angry about the perceived neglect, Courtney had once again become buddy-buddy with Nicole's old rival from junior high, Emily Dooley. Courtney was still hanging out with Emily, but Nicole had finally managed to insert herself into that friendship, forming a triangle she was determined to cut one person out of.

Dropping her backpack and coat on her bed, Nicole hurried into the bathroom she shared with her younger sister, Heather. The girls charged their cordless phone in there when neither one was using

10

it. Creeping through the bathroom toward Heather's adjoining bedroom, Nicole closed the door between them as silently as possible before snatching up the phone, withdrawing into her own room, and shutting that door as well. With a nosy little sister like Heather around, a person couldn't guard her privacy too closely.

Courtney pretended to be stunned to hear from her. "This is Nicole? Nicole *Brewster*? I thought you lost my number."

"Very funny. What are you doing?"

"Math," Courtney said with a sigh. "You?"

"Nothing. I've got homework, but I'll start it after dinner."

"You'll never guess who I talked to today. I was at my locker after school, and he just walked up and said hello."

Nicole had no idea. She could tell from her friend's tone of voice that it was someone she had a crush on, but Courtney hadn't mentioned any crushes since things had fallen apart between her and Jeff Nguyen a couple of months before. "I don't know."

"Jeff!" said Courtney, too impatient to wait for an actual guess. "It was the first time we've talked since . . . you know. And he acted just like nothing had ever happened."

"You mean, like he was still your boyfriend?" Nicole asked, confused.

11

"No. But like we hadn't ever fought, either. Like we were still good friends or something."

"Well, maybe he just wants to bury the hatchet. You guys can't keep ignoring each other forever."

Courtney chuckled, and when she replied her voice was coy. "Oh, I think he wants more than that."

"You mean . . . ?" Nicole asked breathlessly.

"All I'm saying is, he was checking out a lot more than my new sweater. *If* you catch my drift."

Nicole would have had to be unconscious not to. "I can't believe it! So did you tell him off, or what?" After all, Jeff had broken up with Courtney, not the other way around. Courtney had been devastated.

"Now why would I do that?"

"You mean . . . do you still *like* him? How could you not have told me?"

"How could you not have known?" Courtney countered. "Emily knew."

Nicole winced. She *should* have known. She and Courtney had once known even the most minor details of each other's lives. That they had drifted so far apart was sad. But that Emily had already managed to move so far into Nicole's rightful place was downright scary.

"Well, I, uh, I *guessed*," she lied in self defense. "But you should have told me anyway."

"So now you know."

"Well, what are you going to do about it? I mean, are you two going to get back together?"

Courtney laughed. "It's a little early for that. He hasn't even said he wants to go out again yet."

"But you think he will?"

"Just a matter of time," Courtney predicted confidently, sounding like her old self.

Nicole found herself smiling on the other end of the line. Maybe things weren't completely back to normal between her and Courtney, but they were closer than they'd been for a long time. "We'd better hang up," she teased. "He's probably getting a busy signal right now."

"Let him wait," Courtney said. "It's good for guys not to get what they want."

They talked about Jeff awhile longer before Nicole got off the phone, worried that her mother would come upstairs and catch her not doing her homework. "I have to go now, but I'll see you at school tomorrow."

"Meet me by the big trash can at lunch."

"Okay," Nicole agreed, never happier to be bossed around.

It's just like old times, she thought excitedly, hanging up and spreading some homework around as a decoy in case her mother checked. *Me and Courtney on the phone again, meeting for lunch . . . Everything is the same.*

Except for stupid Emily Dooley. The thought wiped the smile off her face. *Why did Courtney have to get wrapped up with her again anyway?*

But unfortunately, Nicole knew why. *That stupid job ruined everything!* Aside from being one of the most humiliating experiences of her entire life, it had made a bad situation with Courtney worse—not to mention totally destroyed her relationship with her cousin Gail.

"Gail," she said with a groan. She still felt awful about telling her parents that Gail had been caught giving away restaurant food, and that their boss was blackmailing her into dating him as a result. Once Gail's parents had learned what was happening, Gail had not only lost her job, she'd also been forbidden to see her college-age boyfriend, Neil.

I had to tell, Nicole reassured herself for the millionth time. *Gail was in over her head. Besides, everyone else thinks I did the right thing.*

Every adult, anyway. But being in the good graces of her parents, no matter how rare and exciting, seemed like cold comfort when her cousin was never going to speak to her again.

Maybe she won't stay mad, Nicole thought hopefully. *Maybe in a month or two she'll realize that I did it for her own good and she'll actually thank me for it. Well . . . maybe in a year or two.*

Nicole sighed.

Oh, who am I kidding? I'd never speak to me again, either.

14

Two

Miguel del Rios checked his face in the rearview mirror, then adjusted his bangs to cover his forehead better. The smudge of ashes Father Sebastian had placed there earlier still showed through his dark hair, but not much.

"So what?" Miguel muttered grumpily as he climbed out of his car and into the student parking lot. "Don't be such a wimp."

Still, he couldn't help feeling conspicuous as he headed toward the main building. Was everyone going to notice? If they did, would they mention it? He could easily wipe the ashes off, the way he had when he was a kid, but there was something holding him back. Miguel had promised God that if his mother got well he'd never doubt him again. And if hiding his faith at school wasn't doubt, exactly, it definitely didn't feel like holding up his end of the bargain.

Ashes are no different than Jenna's cross, he told himself, remembering that no one looked twice at that. *Besides, it's only once a year.*

He yanked the main hall door open, intent on

finding Leah. His crew had worked until after ten o'clock the night before, trying to finish painting a new building, and by the time he'd gotten home and showered it had been too late to call Leah. She'd left a message for him, though, telling him to meet her before first period. He glanced at his watch, then hurried toward her locker, wondering what was so important.

Leah was already there when he arrived, riffling through her books. Sneaking up behind her, he slipped his hands over her eyes. "Guess who?"

"Sergei?" she teased. "Or, wait. It's Rico, right?"

"Sorry. It's your *other* boyfriend," he told her, dropping his hands to nibble her ear. She smelled of soap and warm skin, and he was sorry when she wriggled around to face him, putting an arm's distance between them.

"Where *were* you last night?" she demanded. "Why didn't you call me?"

"Sabrina was determined to finish that building we were working on because there was an early-completion bonus. It was too late to call you when I got home, but the good news is I'll get an extra fifty in my paycheck."

"Oh. That is good," Leah said, with the slightly sour expression that had begun to accompany any mention of Sabrina.

"I'm here now, though," he added quickly. "So what did you want to tell me?"

16

Leah shook her head slightly, then lifted her chin. "I got into Stanford. I found out last night."

Miguel's breath caught in his chest. Adrenaline flooded his body. She was leaving, then. The worst had happened. He gathered himself to congratulate her, to put on a show of happiness.

And then he discovered something he hadn't expected. He *was* happy for her. How could he feel any other way, when she had wanted this so badly?

"Congratulations!" he said, folding her into his arms. "Leah, that's great!"

She held him tightly, nodding silently into his shoulder. He thought he heard her sniff back tears.

"It's going to be okay," he whispered. "We're going to be okay." He'd miss her desperately, of course, but he had always been more optimistic than Leah about their chance of surviving a long-distance relationship.

"I know," she murmured, not sounding a bit convinced.

"We *will*. Just be happy. Because I'm happy for you."

She finally looked up from his shoulder, her eyes full of unshed tears. "I am happy. But—"

"No buts. We're going to make this work. Besides, you know you'll have a fantastic time at Stanford."

Leah nodded. "I know."

Stepping back, she wiped her eyes, then smiled. "Anyway, it's still only February."

"That's the spirit," he told her, smiling in return.

Leah gave him a strange look, then suddenly stepped forward again, stretching a hand toward his forehead. "You have some dirt on your face," she said, preparing to wipe it away.

He caught her wrist before she could. "It's ashes. Today is Ash Wednesday."

"Oh." Dropping her hand, she shrugged, clearly flustered. "I'm sorry. I didn't know."

"It's okay."

"What do they mean?"

"It's kind of a repentance thing, for the first day of Lent," he explained uncomfortably. "The priest puts them on at mass. I used to wipe them off. It's just that this year . . . well . . ."

Her hand reached out again, this time to squeeze one of his. "Don't wipe them off," she said.

He walked her to her homeroom and kissed her outside the door, feeling more sure than he ever had about their relationship. So what if they weren't marrying right away? It didn't change how much they loved each other. Besides, he'd never want to get in the way of Leah's hopes and dreams.

But as he walked to his classroom, he couldn't help wondering about his own hopes and dreams. Leah was on her way to a brilliant future, but what about him? He still didn't even know if he'd get into Clearwater University, let alone how he'd pay for it. There were just so many things to consider.

18

Miguel shook his head. If only his own future were as neatly mapped out as Leah's.

Melanie couldn't wait to get home after school. She closed her front door quietly, not wanting to rouse her father from wherever he'd passed out, and crept up the marble staircase to her bedroom in an agony of suspense.

Her mother's diary was hidden under Melanie's pillows, the bedspread pulled up and smoothed perfectly to deflect any suspicion. The last thing Melanie wanted was for her father to find it—she didn't even want him to *know* about it. Poking her head back out through her doorway, she glanced nervously around the empty second-floor landing, then silently shut the door, pressing until the latch clicked. The chances of her father's making his way upstairs were slim, but Melanie wasn't taking chances.

"Not with this," she whispered, throwing back her pink bedspread and reaching under her pillow. The diary slipped out in her hand, its red leather dark with age, the strap that had once locked the covers dangling uselessly.

Two nights before, she had taken scissors to the strap in her eagerness to read the pages. But the very first words she'd seen had made her reconsider:

This Book Belongs to Tristyn Allen. Keep Out!

Even while the familiar handwriting had tantalized her, its message had forced her to ask if she'd want someone reading her private thoughts after she died. The answer, of course, was no. Reluctantly she'd closed the diary and hidden it away on a shelf of her walk-in closet, behind some scratchy sweaters. Only her exhaustion from her three-day visit with her mother's one sibling, Gwen, had allowed her to fall asleep, though, and all the next day at school she'd barely been able to think of anything else. Cheerleading practice had actually been a welcome distraction.

But when she'd finally arrived home on Tuesday, there had been nothing left to distract her. She had attempted to work on a math assignment, but the whole time, it had seemed the diary was calling her name, making concentration impossible. In the end, she had brought the book to her desk and hidden it in the bottom drawer. She'd thought that having it closer would help curb the urge to read it, but she still thought of nothing else. Every few minutes her hand would drop to the drawer pull . . . and with an effort she'd force it back up. Not until after midnight, after hours of thrashing around in increasingly hot blankets, had she given up, taken the diary to bed, and finally begun reading.

Now, holding it once more, she couldn't wait to pick up where she'd left off. She threw herself down on her stomach and turned eagerly to the page, totally absorbed by the story she was piecing together.

I met Trent for lunch today, but it was awful. We were supposed to go off the grounds, and instead we got in a fight. It seems like every time things start going really well, something like this happens. Like we want to be together, but there's a part of us that doesn't and looks for a reason to end things. All I said was that Lisa saw him talking to Donna Delgado, and he acted like I'd accused him of murder. It's not like I thought there was anything going on, but the way he got so self-righteous actually made me wonder. I mean, he was way too flustered for someone with nothing to hide. So I told him that if he wants to see Donna, it's nothing to me. <u>Less</u> than nothing. I could care. There are about five other guys dying to go out with me. So then he turned it all around and said he never should have talked to Donna, not that there was anything wrong with it, because he had made me jealous. Jealous! I couldn't believe my ears. I told him he would have to make a much bigger impression on me before he made me jealous.

Melanie laughed out loud, stopping abruptly as the unusual sound split the silence. "Oh, that had to hurt," she whispered, savoring her mother's comeback.

From what she had already learned about Trent, Melanie had figured out that her mother had something of a crush-hate relationship with him. The very first entry in the diary had started:

Trent Wheeler asked me to the prom! I never thought I'd actually write anything in this stupid book, but maybe I just didn't have anything to write about before. . . .

None of the entries had dates on them and sometimes days were skipped, which made things pretty confusing, but by slow, careful reading Melanie had deduced that her mother had started writing during the last few weeks of her senior year, specifically a week before the prom. The early pages were full of gossip about the big dance, who was going with whom, and what everyone was wearing. As far as Melanie could tell, her mother was a totally normal teenager. She missed Gwen, who was away at college, but mostly for her usefulness in distracting their overprotective parents. Aside from that, Tristyn was so busy with friends that Gwen's name didn't show up much.

Melanie flipped backward from the page she was on to revisit her mother's description of the prom:

I don't know what to say about the prom, except that I'll never forget it. Everyone was there, and I danced nearly every song. Bambi Walters wore a dress cut down to her navel, which was so typical it wasn't even worth mentioning, but people still talked about it all night. No one was wearing my dress, which was a relief, but someone had Lisa's in a different color. Trent looked adorable in his tux.

22

(*Except for the shoes—what was the story with those?*) *We met Lisa and Paul and the whole gang for dinner. Dinner isn't exactly romantic with that many people around, but everyone else was going in groups so we did too. Paul juggled the silverware and half of it fell on the floor. I honestly thought the waiter was going to throw us out—if Lisa didn't kill Paul first. The dance was better, because even though there were more people there, it felt more private. The only thing I regret is, I wish Trent and I had been dating longer. The prom is a lot of pressure for a first date. Isn't it just like life that a guy you like all year waits until the very last minute to notice?*

Anyway, afterward we went to a party until nearly three in the morning, then a bunch of us had breakfast at the truck stop. Mom and Dad had about a heart attack apiece when I finally got home, but they couldn't do much after I reminded them that they'd said I could stay out as late as I wanted. They said they'd had no idea I would take them so literally. I guess they learned something, didn't they? I hope they forget it before graduation, though, because there will be parties all over town that night. If Trent and I are still seeing each other, we'll probably go together. Otherwise, I'll go with Lisa. It's weird, but I don't know how I feel about Trent now. I was so hot to go out with him for so long, and the prom was fun, but now . . . it's not like I'll die if this is the end. I mean, it's not like we're soul mates.

From the entries she'd read since then, Melanie had concluded the same thing. On the contrary, Tristyn and Trent were a train wreck waiting to happen. One day everything was fine, and they made plans weeks in the future—the next Tristyn didn't care if she never saw him again. Trent seemed ambivalent too, picking flowers for Tristyn on his way to school one day and flirting with random girls the next. Donna Delgado, for instance.

Melanie flipped back to the entry she'd been reading, dying to know if the pair had made it the remaining days to graduation and, if not, who had initiated the breakup. Maybe she wasn't learning anything very important about her mother, but the entire book was juicier than a summer peach.

She had barely found her place, though, when a knock on her door sent her scrambling. She slammed the diary shut and shoved it under the pillows, madly covering everything with her bedspread.

"You in there, Mel?" her father called impatiently.

"Yes. Come on in."

The door opened, and Mr. Andrews regarded her suspiciously. "What are you doing? Sleeping in the middle of the day?"

From the irritation in his voice, she could tell he was sober.

"I just got home. I'm only resting a minute before I start my homework." Her voice was calm but her heart was still pounding. *Of all the days for him to decide not to drink . . .*

"You and I need to talk."

Stepping over the backpack she'd dropped on the floor, he walked to her desk and took a seat. He was wearing old, rumpled khakis, but the mere fact that he had shed his bathrobe showed how serious he was. Melanie sat up straighter on her bed.

"What about?" she asked apprehensively.

"I want to know where you were last weekend. And the weekend before that."

"I told you. Staying at a friend's house."

"What friend?"

Melanie swallowed hard. Was he on to her? She'd gone to a lot of trouble to hide her new involvement with Aunt Gwen. "A girlfriend. What's the big deal?"

"Are you sure it wasn't a boyfriend?"

"Is *that* what you think?" She didn't know whether to laugh or cry at how little her father knew her. The only guys she had dated all school year were Peter and Jesse Jones—and looking back, she didn't know which had been a worse idea. Peter and Jenna were now so tight there wasn't room for a nail file between them, and Jesse . . . Jesse would barely look at her.

"I don't know what to think! You sneak out of here two weekends in a row with the vaguest possible note. As your father, I ought to be entitled to a little more information."

25

"I didn't know you cared. It's not like I'm interrupting your routine."

Mr. Andrews's eyes narrowed. "I don't like your tone. You come on downstairs. It's time to set some new ground rules."

Melanie rolled her eyes. Her father was right to be suspicious, but he couldn't have been more off base. For a moment, she thought of arguing, dying to return to the diary. Then she changed her mind. A lot of time had passed since her father had been in charge of anything, let alone her.

It might be fun to see him try.

Peter's parents were already inside the church, seated in a pew, but he hung back beside the door, hoping to sit with Jenna. She'd been scarce at school the past two days, disappearing to study during lunchtime, and he'd missed her. In fact, he'd barely seen her at all since their date on Sunday night.

The crowd at the door was thinning. Peter glanced nervously back toward his parents, wondering if he should give up and sit down.

No. They have to be coming. It's Ash Wednesday.

The choir wasn't singing at that special evening service, but Peter knew Jenna wouldn't miss the beginning of Lent. Sure enough, a moment later the Conrad family appeared. But the most important member was missing!

"Where's Jenna?" Peter asked, forgetting even to say hello. "Isn't she coming?"

Mrs. Conrad shook her head. "Jenna has a stomachache, so she stayed home tonight."

"Is it anything serious?"

"Yeah. Too much cake for dessert," Maggie quipped, setting Sarah and Allison giggling.

"You girls stop that," Mr. Conrad hushed them, leading his three youngest daughters off toward a pew. Caitlin shot Peter a sympathetic glance, then followed her father as well.

"I don't think it's serious." Mrs. Conrad stayed behind to answer. "It came on so suddenly . . . it's probably just one of those little bugs."

"Do you think she'll be at school tomorrow?"

"Or by Friday at the latest. I'll tell her you said hello." Mrs. Conrad smiled before she walked off to join her family.

Peter's head was a jumble as he hurried to sit with his parents. He had to admit that, up until that moment, he'd been a little afraid that Jenna was avoiding him on purpose, especially after what had happened on Valentine's Day. But now he knew that wasn't the case. Jenna would never be so immature as to skip church just to avoid seeing him. His relief was overwhelming, especially considering he'd just learned his girlfriend was sick.

Her mother said it wasn't serious, though.

On the other hand, if Jenna had still been mad

27

about his kiss with Melanie . . . *That could have been really serious*.

Reverend Thompson walked out to the pulpit, and the congregation became silent as the service began. Peter turned his thoughts from Jenna to Lent, listening to his minister's message of repentance and renewal.

What should I give up this year? Peter wondered, eager to make a sacrifice during the forty days before Easter. *It has to be something good*.

Peter knew a lot of kids, and even some adults, who used Lent as either a kind of divinely enforced diet or an opportunity to break a bad habit. Peter had seen his own years of giving up chocolate or promising not to hit the snooze button on his alarm clock. But this year he wanted his sacrifice to more closely reflect his commitment to God—and it seemed that the best way to do that was to make his loss someone else's gain.

I know! I'll put all my allowance in the Junior Explorers' savings account, to help pay for a day camp.

His parents gave him fifteen dollars each week to cover school lunches and gas for his car, but he was free to spend it on whatever he liked. When he needed cash for a movie or pizza, he simply packed his lunches and rode his bike for a while. He'd done plenty of both to pay for his Valentine's date with Jenna, and that was even after his father had given him some extra cash for the special occasion.

So I'm already in practice, he thought, excited by

the idea. *But this time I won't be doing it for myself, I'll be doing it for the Explorers.*

Ever since Peter had hatched the scheme of holding a summer-long day camp for the kids, he'd been racking his brain for ways to make it happen. They would need a place to hold it, gas for the bus, snacks, art supplies, and things he hadn't even thought of yet. They'd also need plenty of money to pay for it all.

Eight Prime had liked the camp idea enough to put on a Valentine's Day sale of candy and flowers. But unfortunately, Ben Pipkin had stuck them with purple flowers and green suckers, and the sale had been a disaster. Peter wasn't too worried about Eight Prime's first failure, since he was reasonably sure that they could make up their losses by selling the same green suckers on St. Patrick's Day, but if he was going to give the kids a day camp, he'd have to do better than that. He bent his head to pray.

Lord, I give you my allowance with the hope that you'll turn it into something better: the start of a day camp for the Junior Explorers. With your help, that dream will come true.

Peter raised his head, a satisfied smile on his face. He had only just made his pledge, but he couldn't help thinking the hardest part was already done. His promise was well-intentioned, the goal was worthy . . .

Surely camp for the Junior Explorers was just within his reach.

Three

I can't believe we didn't have that stupid geometry quiz after all, Jenna thought as she walked home from school on Thursday.

After the stomachache she'd faked the night before, her mother had been ready to let her stay home, but Jenna had worried about missing the quiz. Mrs. Wilson let them throw out only one bad score per semester, and if Jenna took a zero now she'd have to do well on all the others.

Besides, I was sure to ace this one with all the extra studying I've been doing.

The rest of the class had whined so much about having to take the quiz on the regular Thursday schedule when Monday had been a holiday, though, that Mrs. Wilson had grudgingly postponed it until Friday.

Which means I have to go to school again tomorrow, Jenna thought, dragging her feet along the sidewalk.

She'd have gone anyway. Probably. But it was getting harder and harder to think of reasons to avoid

Peter. Meanwhile, the more she didn't see him, the less she wanted to. She felt stupid about it. She knew she was being a baby. She just couldn't seem to stop.

He'd caught her in the hall that morning, trying to sneak to her locker. Maybe if he'd just apologized one more time . . . Instead he'd given every indication of believing her lame excuse of the night before, saying how glad he was that her stomach was feeling better. She had mumbled something noncommittal, but she couldn't prevent him from following her to class, yammering about his plan to create a day camp the whole time.

At least he's riding his bike for a while, she thought now. *I don't have to invent excuses for not letting him drive me home.*

Up ahead, at the intersection, the light turned green. Jenna ran to catch it, spotting Sarah way up the road as she did. There was no one walking between them, and Jenna continued to trot, closing some of the distance.

Maybe Sarah doesn't have anyone to hang out with this afternoon either, she thought hopefully, remembering the way her little sister had been pestering her and Caitlin for company lately. But the thought made her stop running and grimace instead. *I still haven't asked Caitlin if she's free this weekend. I probably should have done that before I promised Sarah we'd do something with her.*

31

What if her older sister had made other plans? Sarah was going to be upset if Jenna put her off again.

If Cat's busy, then I'll do something with Sarah myself, Jenna decided, resuming a normal pace. *I'll just catch her now and make a plan.*

The obligation couldn't have come at a better time, actually. She'd get Sarah out of her hair and have a custom-made excuse for ignoring Peter, all at the same time.

Gradually the distance between Jenna and Sarah decreased. Jenna could see her sister clearly now, walking along at a snail's pace, her blond head bent over a book. Her sweater made a bright spot of red against the winter sky.

How does she do that? Jenna wondered, watching her sister walk and read at the same time. *It's a miracle she doesn't run into things.*

On the other hand, they'd both made the walk so many times, they knew every obstacle by heart. Except for crossing the streets, there wasn't that much to see. Jenna lagged by only a block now, and she pushed herself to walk faster, wanting to catch her sister. Cars whizzed by, but Jenna was barely aware of them as she concentrated on Sarah. Her sister still didn't seem to realize that Jenna was behind her, and Jenna had a sudden urge to sneak up and give her a thrill. She slowed just enough to move silently, taking long, stealthy steps down the sidewalk.

She was almost close enough to sprint the final

distance when a red car passed her and began steering toward the curb, as if to pick Sarah up.

Who's that? Jenna wondered. The car looked like Jesse's, but why would Jesse stop for Sarah and not her?

Whoever it is, they're going to spoil my surprise, she thought, annoyed. Sarah would turn to see the car and see Jenna at the same time.

But Sarah was so engrossed in her book, she didn't even seem to realize a car was pulling over. It hadn't slowed much, either. Was it stopping after all? Jenna stopped to watch curiously as the car continued toward the curb.

It can't be stopping; it's going too fast. That driver had better straighten out the wheel or—

Before she could finish her thought, the car jumped the curb, careening diagonally across the grass toward the sidewalk.

Sarah! Jenna screamed, but no sound came out. She felt as paralyzed as in a nightmare as the car sped toward her sister.

Sarah snapped her head up, alerted to the danger by the sound of the approaching car. She spun around, but it was too late. Jenna caught only a glimpse of her sister's disbelieving face before the car hit her at full speed, tossing her up like a toy into somebody's front yard.

Jenna screamed out loud this time, the sound ripped from her throat. "Sarah!"

The car slowed, changed direction, then rolled back onto the pavement and drove off. Sarah lay motionless in the grass where she had landed, her sweater bright against the green, one bare leg twisted up beneath her.

For a moment Jenna was unable to move. Nothing seemed real—not the car disappearing down the street, not her sister's crumpled body. Was Sarah dead? Was it possible? Jenna took a weak step forward, then collapsed sobbing on the sidewalk, too afraid to look.

"Help! Help us!" she screamed hysterically. "Somebody help us. Please!"

People ran out of the surrounding houses. A blue car stopped at the curb, its young male driver bounding out and up the lawn to Sarah.

"Call 911!" Jenna cried, choking on her tears. "Call my mother!"

A gray-haired woman rushed over to her, crouching down on the sidewalk to take Jenna's hand. "I already called 911," she said. "What's your mother's number?"

But Jenna couldn't remember. She pushed her backpack into the woman's hands, relying on her to find some ID. "Sarah," she whimpered, struggling back to her feet. A crowd had gathered around her sister, blocking her from view. "Sarah!"

Jenna staggered forward, barely aware of her legs underneath her. Someone supported her by one arm, helping her up the lawn. The crowd parted as she drew near and dropped to her knees by her sister. The man from the blue car was on his knees too, beginning CPR on Sarah's motionless body.

Sarah's face was white as a canvas, a trickle of blood like red paint at one corner of her mouth. Her eyes were closed, as if to block out the sight Jenna couldn't, and the bent leg resting beneath her was broken. The angle alone was enough to bring the bile to Jenna's throat, even before she saw the blood and shattered bone pushing through the skin from inside.

"I can't do this," the CPR guy said, rocking back on his heels. "I think her ribs must be broken, the way they're moving around. It's like a section of her chest is loose."

"No, don't stop," Jenna begged.

"I have to." His face twisted with fear and reluctance. "I'm afraid I'll puncture something."

Jenna looked desperately at the rest of the crowd, then back down at her sister. "Please don't let her die," she sobbed, leaning over until the top of her head touched Sarah's sweater. "Don't just let her die."

A blast from a siren split the air, unexpectedly near.

"Here's the ambulance!" someone shouted. "Everyone out of the way!"

There was a rush of movement as people scrambled to clear a path, but Jenna didn't budge until a woman lifted her gently away from Sarah and onto her feet.

"Don't let her die," Jenna begged, blinded by her own tears.

Two medics rushed in with cases of emergency equipment. Soon Jenna was moved back even farther to give them room to work.

"I'm her sister," she whimpered helplessly. "Oh, please, God, don't let her die."

The medics seemed to move in slow motion, checking Sarah over.

"I've got a pulse," one said, "but it's weak." He slapped a clear plastic mask over Sarah's face, forcing air into her lungs with the attached squeeze bulb.

"Internal bleeding," his partner replied, beginning an IV. Turning his head, he addressed the ambulance driver. "Get me a backboard and collar, stat. We've got to get her in fast or this is all over."

Jenna heard the screams coming out of her mouth as if from far away. They were a sound she no longer controlled. She slid out of the woman's hands and down to the cold grass, the whole scene spinning around her.

The driver brought the equipment and worked with the men a minute. Then she walked over and took Jenna by the shoulders, her face swimming in and out of focus. "Stop it," she said, squeezing Jenna's arms. "I know it's hard, but if you want to help your sister, you have to be strong. We don't need two patients right now."

Somehow Jenna managed to stop screaming, gulping for air instead. Over the driver's shoulder, she saw Sarah on a rolling stretcher being loaded into the ambulance. "I'm going with her," she said, jerking up to her feet.

Blood surged from her head in a sickening rush, making her cling to the woman for support. The driver half walked, half dragged her to the rear of the ambulance and pushed her up onto a bench beside the stretcher. The men were already inside, tending to Sarah.

If possible, Sarah looked even worse than she had on the grass. The oxygen mask and IV were still in place, and now a hard plastic collar braced her neck while a strap across her forehead held her motionless to the bed. A blanket covered the long padded lump where her body should have been.

The double doors slammed shut with a bang, the siren wailed, and the ambulance sped away. It all seemed like a dream until Jenna felt a painful pressure on her left arm.

"Just routine," the medic in the middle of the bench explained as Jenna turned toward the source of her discomfort. Somehow he had slapped on a blood-pressure cuff without her even realizing it.

"What are you doing? I'm fine," she quavered,

hearing her voice betray her words. "Please help my sister instead."

"We're doing all we can for her." He removed the cuff and, taking a blanket from behind him, wrapped it around Jenna's shoulders. "Better?"

She hadn't even realized she was cold. How much colder Sarah must be! Struggling out of the blanket, Jenna tried to spread it over her sister, but the man held her back.

"If you want to help, then do what I tell you," he said, rewrapping Jenna in the blanket. "You've had a big shock and you need to calm down. Just sit here and don't move."

"That's right," the other medic said curtly, leaning over Sarah as if to protect her. "For God's sake, don't help us."

Jenna stared, surprised by his tone, and fresh tears poured down her cheeks. She pulled the blanket so tight she could barely breathe as she rocked back and forth to her sobs. All she wanted was for someone to tell her that Sarah would be all right. She couldn't die. Not now. Not like this.

But the longer Jenna kept her eyes closed, the more afraid she was to open them. There was no other sound but the siren. Maybe Sarah had died already.

The back doors were yanked open abruptly, flooding the ambulance with light. They had arrived at the hospital. A new medic reached in and handed Jenna out, while others grabbed Sarah's stretcher and snapped down the wheels. The carport outside the emergency room was suddenly swarming with people.

"Let's move!" a doctor barked. "This one goes straight to Trauma."

The mechanical glass doors of the hospital opened as the crew wheeled Sarah toward them. Jenna stumbled after her sister, but inside a nurse held her back while Sarah's group continued down the hall.

"I'm sorry, but you can't go with her," she said as Jenna strained to follow. "They're going to operate."

"But I have to be there! I have to—"

"I need you to come in here and have a seat." The woman's face was sympathetic as she led Jenna into a small, darkened room with several chairs and a small table. "Let's try to calm down."

"I don't need to calm down. I need—"

"Take a few deep breaths," the nurse urged gently.

Jenna gulped down some air. "Now can I see my sister?"

The woman shook her head. "Not yet. You can see her when she's out of surgery."

"But she could die in there!"

The nurse patted her back but didn't deny it. Jenna felt things start to spin again.

"Jenna! Jenna, what happened?" Mrs. Conrad cried, appearing in the doorway. Her auburn hair was windblown and her eyes were wild with fear. "Someone called and said there had been an accident."

"Sarah got hit by a car!" Jenna bolted out of the chair to reach her mother's arms. "She was just walking, and it ran right off the road."

"They took her in for surgery. Your other daughter wasn't hurt, but she's pretty shaken up." The nurse nodded toward Jenna.

"Where is the doctor?" Mrs. Conrad demanded, holding Jenna tight. "Who can tell me what's going on? How badly is Sarah hurt?"

"It's bad," Jenna wailed. "Oh, Mom, I'm so scared."

The next hour was a blur. Someone ran in to ask about Sarah's medical history and have Mrs. Conrad sign some forms. Jenna was given a sedative. Mr. Conrad arrived in the little room shortly after that. While a team of doctors worked to save Sarah in another part of the hospital, Jenna tried to explain how the accident had happened. A doctor came in and made a report. Sarah had a broken leg, broken ribs, and severe internal bleeding due to a ruptured spleen. The only way to keep her from bleeding to death was to perform an emergency splenectomy, which was already under way.

"I can't believe this is happening," Mrs. Conrad

whispered when the doctor left them. "All we can do is pray."

Mr. Conrad put an arm around his wife. Jenna's hand drifted to the gold cross around her neck just as a policeman walked into the room.

"I'm Officer Rice," he said, pointing to his badge. "Are you Sarah Conrad's parents?"

"Yes." Mr. Conrad rose to his feet.

"I know this is a hard time for you folks, but I thought you'd want to know we caught the driver. College girl out of CU, so far under the influence I'm surprised she could find her keys. We have a number of witnesses, and one of them got her plates."

"She was drunk?" Mrs. Conrad asked angrily. "Is she under arrest?"

"Oh yes," said the man. "Absolutely. Driving under the influence, felony hit-and-run, and that's just for starters. I wouldn't want to be her when she sobers up. They're going to prosecute this to the limit."

Mr. Conrad sank back into his chair.

"I understand you were at the scene too?" the officer asked Jenna. She saw his mouth move, but his voice faded in and out, making the words hard to understand.

"Yes," she heard herself answer. Her tongue felt thick in her mouth.

"I'll need to get your statement, but we can do that later. It's already an open-and-shut case."

She nodded. "Later."

Then somehow Peter appeared. Jenna didn't ask how he'd found her as she melted into his arms.

"It's okay," he told her over and over, his lips just brushing her ear. "It's going to be okay."

But he didn't know that. How could he? Jenna clung to him anyway, wanting to believe those reassuring words.

At last another doctor appeared, wearing green surgical scrubs. A mask had been pulled down around his neck, and what looked like a paper shower cap covered most of his short black hair. "Hello, I'm Dr. Malone," he said. "I've been in surgery with your daughter, and I'm assuming charge of her care."

"How is she?" Jenna's parents asked in unison, leaping to their feet.

The doctor took a deep breath, clasping and unclasping his long hands. "She's unconscious and very critical. We removed the spleen, but she lost a lot of blood. We're replacing that, and if we can stabilize her, we'll run a CT scan. In the meantime, we've got her on a ventilator, and we've strapped up that flail chest. The leg will have to wait a little longer."

Jenna didn't know what a flail chest was, but she barely cared after that one horrifying "if."

"*If* you can stabilize her?" Mrs. Conrad repeated, stuck on the same awful word. "You mean *when* you stabilize her, right? Sarah's going to make it."

The doctor's dark eyes met hers. "I wish I could

say yes. The truth is, I don't know. She's extremely critical."

"No," Jenna heard herself insist, trying to rise from her chair. Her legs refused to obey her. "She's going to live!"

Dr. Malone walked over and laid one hand on her shoulder. "I'll do my best," he promised.

"No, not your best. You have to save her!"

Jenna couldn't seem to get her feet underneath her. She strained against Peter's arms, desperate to stand up. Why was he fighting her? And why was the room suddenly so hot?

Too hot. Everything swam out of focus. The doctor's face dissolved last of all, melting into a warm brown blur. Jenna felt her body go limp.

Then everything went black.

Four

"Oh, no!" several members of Eight Prime gasped. "Poor Jenna!" said Nicole. "How awful!"

"But her sister's going to recover," Leah said quickly. "Right?"

Peter kept his eyes on the table, determined not to cry. There was a lump in his throat the size of an egg, but he managed to speak around it. "They don't know yet. She's in pretty bad shape."

"Poor Jenna," Nicole repeated. "No wonder she's not here today."

"At least *she* didn't get hurt," said Ben. "It could have been even worse."

"I'm not sure Jenna sees it that way." Peter blinked hard several times before he finally looked up. With Ben's help, he had managed to gather Eight Prime at a corner table in the busy cafeteria—all but Jenna, of course, who hadn't left the hospital since she'd arrived with Sarah the day before. "I think in a lot of ways she would rather it was her."

"What good would that do?" Melanie asked. "She's just upset."

"She's *very* upset," said Peter. "And that's why I wanted to get everyone together. Jenna needs our support right now. She'll need it until this thing is all over."

However it turns out, he almost added, but he couldn't bring himself to say it.

The doctors had worked on Sarah late into the night, but her condition hadn't changed—except for the announcement that she was officially in a coma. She was so critical that only her parents had been allowed to see her. Peter wanted more than anything to believe Sarah would live, but he'd seen the expressions on the doctors' faces. And on the Conrads'.

"Well, of course we're going to support her!" Leah put her hand over Miguel's, speaking for them both. "We'd do anything for Jenna."

"We should all go to the hospital after school," said Nicole, turning to Jesse. "Can I ride with you?"

"Sure. I can take a couple more, too, if anyone else needs a ride."

Peter shook his head. "I don't think today's so good. No one's allowed to see Sarah yet, and Jenna may not be ready. Tomorrow would be better. And since it's not a school day, we can spread ourselves out a little instead of all showing up at once."

"That would be better," Melanie agreed. "She probably doesn't need a big crowd."

Everyone at the table began making plans for

the Saturday visit—who'd drive with whom and when—but now that the important things had been said, Peter found his attention drifting away, back to Jenna at the hospital.

He knew Sarah's condition was dire, and Jenna was right to be upset, but the hopeless way she was acting was really starting to scare him. He had stayed with her at the hospital until nearly midnight the night before, and once she'd come out of her faint she had been a lot calmer. In a way, though, her calm had been even more disconcerting than her hysterics. She'd sat like a stone in her chair, staring blindly straight ahead. The only time she had spoken was when someone asked her a question. The only time she'd looked up was when a doctor walked into the room. It was as if the worst had already happened.

As if she had no hope at all.

"Shouldn't we be getting home?" Nicole asked anxiously, pointing to the big tower clock in the mall. "It's getting kind of late."

"You call this late?" Emily scoffed. "I'd hate to party with you."

Courtney laughed appreciatively, marking a point for Emily on an imaginary blackboard.

I hate doing anything *with you*, Nicole thought sullenly, dropping back as her so-called friends turned down a side aisle. *There aren't even any good stores in this part. Not that you would know the difference.*

For all Emily's wardrobe improvements since junior high, she still liked some pretty lame stuff. *It's a good thing she has Courtney to help her shop for the prom.*

Which was what they were all supposedly there to do. Although the prom was still two months off, it only seemed smart to check out the new styles early. When Nicole had agreed to go, it had sounded incredibly fun. She could have done without Emily's presence, of course, but after the horrors of Wienerageous, a normal afternoon's shopping had seemed like a bit of heaven.

Of course that was all before she'd heard about Sarah Conrad. Nicole looked at her watch, exasperated, as Courtney and Emily slowed to peek into a candy store. It was barely five o'clock. If she left now, she could still stop by the hospital and talk to Jenna for a few minutes. She could if she had a car, that was. And if Peter hadn't told them all to wait until the next day.

"Did you see Jeff checking me out at lunch?" Courtney asked Emily.

"Oh, definitely," said Emily, sucking up.

"You'd have seen it too, if you hadn't been hanging out with the stupid God Squad," Courtney accused, glancing back over her shoulder at Nicole.

"I'm sorry, but it was a *little* important," Nicole returned sarcastically.

"Oh, right. Poor Jenna," Courtney said flippantly.

"Her problems are so much more important than mine."

"This one is." How could Courtney even compare guy trouble to having a sister in a coma? For a moment, Nicole thought her friend would argue anyway. Then her green eyes softened.

"Well . . . maybe," she admitted. "But I'm tired of talking about it." With a toss of her red hair, she turned her attention back to Emily.

We never even talked about it! Nicole wanted to scream.

In a way, that was the worst part. Sarah was practically all Nicole had been able to think about since lunchtime, but after hearing the bare basics Courtney and Emily had changed the subject, not interested. Nicole knew that Jenna wasn't their friend, but was expecting a little compassion so unreasonable? What if Sarah died? How would Jenna stand it?

"I always thought Jeff and I would get back together," Courtney was telling Emily. "I never understood why we broke up in the first place."

"You know how guys are." The way Emily tried to sound like such an expert made Nicole want to puke. "They never appreciate anything until they lose it."

"That's right." Courtney stopped suddenly and pointed through a window at a slinky, sequined number in her new trademark color: apple green.

"I'll bet he'd appreciate me wearing that! A girl could make an entrance in that."

A girl could glow in the dark in that, thought Nicole, looking at her watch again.

"Listen, I'm going to go," she blurted out. "There's a bus in a few minutes, and I'll just take it home."

"Since when do you know the bus schedules?" Courtney asked, making a face.

"Since . . . I just remembered, all right?" No way did she want to explain how she'd memorized the entire bus schedule riding back and forth to Wiener-ageous every day. "I saw what I came to see. Besides, I have a lot to do at home."

"Like what?" Emily asked with a smirk.

Like get away from you.

"Things," Nicole said tensely. "I'll call you later, Court."

They were talking about Jeff again before Nicole was even out of hearing, and on the bus ride home she wondered if she'd done the right thing. Would it have killed her to stay?

Yes. It would have. How could she go on pretending things were normal when she was worried sick? *If they had at least listened . . .*

But all Courtney had wanted to do was talk about Jeff.

Guy would have listened, Nicole thought, staring out the bus window. The idea surprised her. What on Earth had made her think of Guy Vaughn?

Probably Courtney going on about Jeff.

Nicole had met Guy on a double date arranged by Courtney. Her best friend and Jeff had been hot and heavy at the time, and Jeff had wanted to double with his good friend Guy. But once Courtney had found out that Guy went to Ozarks Prep, a Christian private school, she'd decided the only person crazy enough to go out with him was Nicole.

That first date had been a disaster. And since Nicole had thought she'd been stuck with the loser, she'd been absolutely outraged when Guy said she wasn't a serious person and he didn't want to see her again. For a while, all she could think about was revenge; then her parents had dumped her into a Christmas-break Bible class where Guy was an advisor. The two of them hadn't exactly made up, but by the time Nicole had walked away, she'd been content not to break his heart after all. Later, she'd run into him at the Hearts for God rally in Los Angeles. He'd been unexpectedly cool performing with his band, not to mention nice when she'd been mourning the death of her modeling dreams. And he'd stopped by Wienerageous once, too, just to visit her. . . .

If Guy were around, he'd understand what I'm going through. In fact, he'd be worried himself, because he'd met Jenna in Los Angeles. With everything that had happened between them, Nicole didn't really know how she felt about Guy, but he was certain to be more sympathetic than Courtney.

"I'm going to call him," she said, startled when the man in the bus seat two rows ahead turned to see who she was talking to. Nicole forced a weak smile, then slid down with her cheeks blazing.

The moment she got home, she ran straight to her room and began digging through her desk. She still had Guy's phone number somewhere from that December Bible class. And although she had never called him before, she'd never had a reason this good before, either.

"Here it is!" she said, pulling the green Teen Extreme folder out from under the junk in the bottom drawer. A moment later she was dialing the phone. "Be there," she begged as it rang, hoping he would pick up himself.

"Hello?" a male voice answered at last.

"Guy?" Nicole said uncertainly. "Hi. It's Nicole. Nicole Brewster," she added after an uncomfortably long pause.

"Right. I just . . . How are you, Nicole?" He was obviously stunned to hear from her, but at least he knew who she was.

"All right. Well. Not so good." She took a deep breath. "Do you remember Jenna Conrad? You met her in L.A., and she totally loved your band."

"Sure."

"Well, her little sister Sarah got hit by a car yesterday right in front of her."

"That's terrible!" he cried, genuinely dismayed. "Is she okay? I mean her sister. Did she . . . ?"

"Not yet," said Nicole, choking up. "But she's real bad. No one knows if she'll make it."

"What can I do? Anything? Is there anything at all?"

Nicole hadn't expected the question. "I, uh, I don't know. What can any of us do? A bunch of us are going by the hospital tomorrow, just to be there for Jenna, but—"

"I'll drive you," he volunteered. "Let me pick you up."

"Um, I guess so. If you want to."

"Unless you don't want me around," he added, a little stiffly.

"Of course I do. If I didn't, would I have called you?"

"Then I'm there. I'm right there. And if you need a shoulder, or Jenna needs a shoulder, or just . . . whatever I can do. I'm serious."

She knew he was. And the relief of finally finding someone she could lean on almost made her cry.

"Jenna? You don't look good," Caitlin said in a quiet, tired voice.

Jenna stared. After what they'd all been through, did people expect her to look her best?

"I don't *feel* good," she retorted. "None of us looks great."

On the other side of Caitlin, Maggie tugged nervously on one of her auburn curls while a tear-streaked Allison squirmed in her ICU waiting-room chair. Maggie leaned across Caitlin.

"Do you want me to go get Mom?" she asked Jenna worriedly.

"You *can't* get Mom," Jenna said. "If we were allowed in with Sarah, I'd be in there myself."

"But we're going to be any minute," Allison told them. "Mom said."

"Mom said maybe," Caitlin reminded her. "We'll have to wait and see."

"If we do get in, it's one at a time and I'm going first," Jenna said, not caring whether that was fair. "I've been here the longest, and I'm going first."

The younger girls both regarded her with red-rimmed eyes but, amazingly, didn't argue.

"Sure, Jenna," Caitlin said quickly. "That's fine."

Jenna turned away from her sisters and refocused her attention on the wall clock over the nurses' station. The hands and numbers were black on a stark white face, and watching the second hand make its rounds was the only thing that helped her stay calm. Every completed trip was a minute longer that Sarah had lived—and the longer Sarah held on, the better her chances had to be. Or at least that was what Jenna had decided to believe.

No, that has to be right, she thought, unwilling to accept any other answer.

Sarah couldn't die, because if she did it would be Jenna's fault.

I should have yelled. I should have warned her. If I had just caught up instead of fooling around, I could have pushed her out of the way.

She could have if she'd realized that the car was going to run off the road, anyway. But she hadn't until it was already careening across the sidewalk. There had been no time for a push, and even if she had managed the scream that had stuck in her throat, Sarah probably couldn't have leapt to safety. In her mind, Jenna could still see her sister being flung through the air, more like a doll than a person. Everything had just happened so fast. . . .

Jenna dropped her head into her hands, barely noticing the tears that wet her palms. It felt like she'd been crying all her life. Her long hair spilled in front of her, nearly to the floor, as she hid her face from her sisters. She had never felt so guilty, so completely responsible for something in her life. It did no good to tell herself that there was nothing she could have done, that if she hadn't been there Sarah would have been hit in the same way. It did no good, because she still couldn't shake the real source of her guilt: the knowledge that she'd failed Sarah long before the accident.

I should have paid more attention to her, she berated herself, sniffing back bitter tears. *Does she even know how much I love her? What if she dies without waking up? I may never get to tell her.*

She hated herself now for not letting Sarah help her and Caitlin walk dogs the week before. What business was it of Jenna's anyway? Caitlin was the one with the dog-walking business, and she'd said it was fine. But Jenna had been selfish, wanting Sarah to stay home so that she and Caitlin could talk more freely about their upcoming Valentine's dates. Later, after Jenna's date had turned into disaster, she'd been so wrapped up in herself that she hadn't even gone to church with her family for Lent. Worse, she had lied to get out of it.

Her heart contracted suddenly, as if squeezed by a cold hand. Was that why the accident had happened? Was God punishing her?

No, she thought, massaging her aching temples. *God doesn't work that way.*

But in her mind she saw Sarah flying through the air, broken like a stick, and despair almost shut down her senses.

Why not just admit it? She wasn't sure how God worked anymore.

"Jenna?"

Her father's voice took her by surprise. Jenna jerked her head up to see him standing in front of her, still wearing yesterday's clothes.

"Can we see her?" she asked desperately. "I'm not going home until I see her."

Mr. Conrad held out a hand to help pull her to her feet. "You can see her," he said gently. "And then you *are* going home. Your mom will stay here by herself tonight."

She followed her father silently, waiting to argue until after she'd seen Sarah. She hadn't left the hospital since the accident, and she didn't plan to leave it until Sarah came home with her. Or until . . .

Tears were already streaming down her face as her father led her through the swinging door into the intensive care unit. There were other beds, with green curtains pulled around them, but Jenna kept her eyes on her father's back as she followed him to the bed in the farthest, quietest corner.

The bed was high, with silver rails. Mrs. Conrad sat in the only chair beside it, overshadowed by the bank of equipment behind her. Jenna's steps faltered as she took in the awful scene. She'd thought she was prepared, but it was one thing to know Sarah was on a ventilator and another to actually see the machine pumping, counting out every breath. There was one of those jumping-green-line heart monitors, too, and a couple of IV stands with bags of clear fluid. Jenna found her eyes glued to Sarah's digitized heartbeat, remembering the movies she'd seen in which that line had gone suddenly flat.

"Come in, but be quiet," her mother whispered, waving her over to the bed. "Dr. Malone said you girls can only stay a minute."

Jenna glanced at her mother's drawn face, then at the bed, her feet still stuck to the floor. Was that Sarah? That small lump under the hospital blanket? From where Jenna stood, she could barely make out the top of her sister's blond head. With an effort, she forced herself forward, took hold of a rail, and walked along it until she was even with Sarah's face.

"Don't pull on that," her mother said worriedly, jumping up. "Don't wiggle that bed at all."

Jenna barely heard her in her shock at what she saw. "How did she get so bad?" she wailed. "What happened to her face?"

Sarah's eyes were still closed, but her once-pale lids were now the dark purple of bruises. Her face, so white after the accident, had become blotchy and swollen, a bruise spreading outward from the corner of her mouth where the blood had been.

"She bit the inside of her cheek," her mother explained. "And the rest, well . . . there's just a lot of trauma, Jenna. An impact like Sarah experienced—"

Jenna shook her head to end the explanation. She didn't need her mother to tell her about the impact. She saw it every time she closed her eyes.

"What about the leg?" she asked huskily.

Carefully her mother pulled back the blanket.

Sarah's legs were bare beneath the hem of a too-large hospital gown. One was pale, skinny, a little scratched up. But the other . . .

Jenna squeezed her eyes shut, feeling her stomach rise toward her throat. The break had been so complicated that the doctors hadn't set it with a cast. Instead, they'd drilled pins into the good ends of Sarah's bone, letting the long ends protrude through the flesh and connect to a metal frame outside. A bandage covered the skin of the immediate area, but the rest of the leg was bare and black with bruises, swollen down to the foot.

When Jenna opened her eyes, her mother had covered Sarah again and was arranging the blanket, but one of Sarah's hands stuck out from under the edge. Jenna reached to hold it, only to find it fastened to some sort of board. An IV punctured the skin of the back, the needle affixed with tape that went around the whole hand. Jenna faltered, then squeezed the tips of Sarah's fingers instead, terrified by how cold and lifeless they felt.

"Oh, Sarah," she choked out, unable to hold back her tears any longer. "Sarah, I'm so sorry."

Sobs shook her body. If Sarah was aware of her surroundings, Jenna knew she was probably making things worse, but she found herself helpless to stop. It was all just too much.

"Okay," her mother whispered, slipping a gentle arm around her. "That's enough." There were tears in her voice too, as she led Jenna away from the bed. "Time for you to go home and get some sleep. You've done as much as you can here, and it won't help Sarah if you get sick. Go get some rest, and tomorrow you can come back."

"I don't want to leave her," Jenna said stubbornly.

"She doesn't even know you're here, Jenna, and I'm not going to argue with you."

Still crying, Jenna followed her father as he led her from the room. "I won't be able to sleep," she protested the second they reached the hall. "I'll just be lying there, awake. How is that going to help anyone?"

Her father lovingly smoothed her hair. "It might help if you pray."

Jenna opened her mouth, then shut it again, exhausted and confused.

Two days before, she'd have prayed with all her heart. But in the hours since Sarah's accident, it seemed her prayers had turned against her too. Half-finished and weak, full of doubt and distraction, fragile, lame little things . . .

Could prayers like that even make it off the ground?

Five

"I can't believe we're here again," Leah said, parking her father's car in the hospital lot on Saturday morning. "Is this group jinxed or what?"

"At least we drove at a normal speed this time," joked Miguel.

"At least I'm conscious this time," Melanie said from the backseat. "I'll bet *my* last ride here was faster than yours."

Leah tried to smile despite the creeping dread inside her. The last time Eight Prime had all assembled at the hospital, Melanie had been rushed there in an ambulance after a failed cheerleading stunt.

"Don't forget that I rode with Jesse last time," Ben told Melanie. "I'll bet you wouldn't have beat us if we'd started at the same time."

"Maybe not." Melanie made a face that Leah couldn't read.

They climbed out of the car and started walking toward the building, Melanie carrying the fancy box of chocolates they'd all chipped in to buy.

"Pretty soon I'll be driving you guys around," Ben

said proudly, walking backward to see their faces. "I'm turning sixteen next month, and my dad's going to start teaching me tomorrow. Finally!"

"When are you turning sixteen, Melanie?" asked Miguel.

"Not until August," she said with a sigh.

Inside the lobby, Leah watched as Miguel turned a slow half-circle, trying to get his bearings. "The children's ward is on the second floor, but—"

"She's still in intensive care," Leah finished for him. "Fifth floor. I checked with Peter before I left."

They all trooped to the elevator, where Ben pressed the button extra hard. Melanie rolled her eyes.

"What time should I come for you this afternoon?" Leah asked Miguel on the ride up. He was going to walk to work from the hospital, and she was planning to pick him up when he was through.

He shrugged. "Better let me call you. Sabrina may want me overtime again."

She wants you, all right, Leah thought jealously, unable to stop worrying that Sabrina's interest in Miguel was more than strictly professional. Now that she knew for sure she was going to Stanford, Leah was doing her best to come to terms with leaving Miguel behind for a while. She'd have felt a lot better about their chances for a happy reunion, though, if he hadn't been working with Sabrina.

The elevator doors slid open.

"Fifth floor," Melanie announced.

"Look at the people!" said Ben.

After Peter's warnings about keeping things low-key and not all showing up at once, Leah was completely unprepared for the crowd in the tiny fifth-floor waiting room. All the chairs were full, leaving a number of people standing. They milled about, talking in low voices, like guests at a funeral. Spotting Jenna and Peter in a corner, Leah headed that way.

"Hi, you guys," Peter greeted them as they approached. His face was somber, his voice weighted down with the seriousness of the occasion.

Jenna looked right through them, as if unsure who they were. Her eyes were bloodshot and swollen from crying, her thick hair barely combed. Leah had always thought Jenna was pretty, but that day she looked like the heroine in the last few scenes of her own horror movie.

"Jenna!" Leah said, rushing forward to hug her. "Is Sarah any better?"

Jenna gave her a weak hug back, then withdrew from her grasp, a slight shake of the head her only answer.

"We brought you some candy," Melanie said, walking nearer to hand it over.

"It's from all of us," Ben added.

Jenna smiled faintly, but it was Peter who ended up taking the box. "Ooh, chocolate," he said, lifting the lid. "Which one are you going to eat first? I'll bet that one's a caramel," he added, pointing.

Jenna looked vaguely sick. "Maybe later," she whispered.

Peter put the lid back on the box and gave his friends a helpless look. "Sarah's still in a coma. She's not responding at all."

"I'm sorry," Miguel told Jenna. Melanie and Ben nodded their sympathy.

"At least she's not any worse," Leah said, trying for some spark of life from Jenna. "There's still hope. Right?"

"Right!" Peter said immediately.

But Jenna only stared at the floor, eyes glazed with despair. Leah could barely believe that the zombie in front of her now was the spirited girl she had known since September, the eternal optimist, the Eight Prime member most likely to be cheerful.

"We're here for you, Jenna," Leah whispered, her heart breaking for her friend. She caught Jenna's hands and held them tight. "Every one of us. Don't you give up now."

Jenna nodded dully, then turned her head away.

She didn't look like she had even a drop of hope left.

I should have gone with Leah, Melanie thought, glancing uncomfortably around the ICU waiting room. Miguel had stayed only a short time before heading off to work. Leah and Ben had lasted longer but had said their good-byes several minutes before. *I don't know what I thought I'd accomplish by staying.*

Jenna was barely talking to anyone, even Peter, and the rest of the people in the room were total strangers, although Peter had identified them for her earlier. All Jenna's sisters were there, including Mary Beth, home from college. They were clearly worried, too, but not like Jenna; Jenna was downright grim. Her parents seemed the calmest as they talked to the other adults, most of them members of their church. Melanie tried to imagine what it would be like to have such a built-in second family, but she didn't get very far.

I barely even know what it's like to have a regular family.

A nice-looking couple hugged Mr. and Mrs. Conrad, then, on their way to the elevator, walked past the chairs where Jenna, Peter, and Melanie were sitting.

"Keep your chin up, Jenna," the woman urged. "Faith works miracles."

Jenna smiled a little, but the comment didn't really seem to touch her. Melanie, on the other hand, shifted self-consciously in her chair. Not everyone in the room went to the Conrads' church—there was a neighbor or two, someone from Mr. Conrad's work, and, of course, the nurses—but it seemed like everyone shared the same view. Everyone except her, that was. Was she the only nonbeliever in the hospital, or did it only feel that way?

She was distracted from the question by the opening of the elevator doors. The exiting couple stepped in and Jesse stepped out, his arms loaded with flowers and a paper shopping bag. He glanced around and then headed toward the three of them.

"Jenna. Hi," he said softly, setting his bag on the floor. "I'm so sorry about what happened."

Jenna nodded. "Thanks."

"Here. These are for you." Crouching down, he divided the huge bunch of flowers into three separate bouquets and put one into her hands.

"These others are for Sarah and your mother," he explained. "I just wanted to do *something*."

A tear slipped down Jenna's cheek, but she didn't seem to notice. "Sarah's not allowed to have flowers. I don't know what we'd put them in anyway."

"I've got it covered." Using his free hand, he pulled a simple glass vase from the shopping bag. "There are three of them. I figured you'd need them, but I couldn't carry three vases full of water."

"That's so sweet." The wistful words left Melanie's mouth before she had a chance to censor them.

Jesse gave her a startled glance, as if waiting for the "but" that was sure to follow.

"It is sweet," Jenna said. "I wish Sarah could have them."

"You never know," he said. "Maybe tomorrow."

Peter signaled Jesse with a slight, worried shake of his head.

"Or the next day," Jesse added quickly. "How about I go find some water and put them on the nurses' desk for now? When Sarah's ready for them, they'll be ready for her."

Jenna nodded mutely, and Jesse walked off with the flowers and vases.

"Wow, that's so unlike him," Melanie said when he had gone.

"How so?" Peter asked. "It seems just like him to me."

"It does?"

Peter shrugged. "Why not?"

The three of them sat in silence, Melanie wondering how Peter had arrived at such a high opinion of Jesse, until Jesse came back with two full vases. Melanie watched as he set one on the nurses' station and offered the other to Mrs. Conrad. He disappeared again after that, finally returning with the third vase and placing it on the floor in front of Jenna.

"I bet they'll all still be in bloom when Sarah wakes up," he told her, earning another wan smile.

Then Peter started whispering to Jenna, and Jesse took the empty seat on Melanie's other side.

"There, uh, sure are a lot of people here," he said awkwardly.

"Mostly from their church." If he was going to be civil, she supposed she could do the same. "And Jenna's oldest sister."

She pointed out Mary Beth, who was talking to Maggie on the other side of the room. The pair looked like young and old versions of the same person with their freckled faces and tight auburn curls, but whereas Melanie imagined that Maggie probably took plenty of teasing for those distinctive features, Mary Beth had grown into hers.

"I figured she was related," Jesse said. He twiddled his thumbs in his lap, turning his body slightly so only Melanie could see. "And now . . . ?"

"Yeah." Melanie had no idea what to do either. She really wanted to help, but Jenna barely even seemed aware of her presence. It was as if grief and all the commotion in the room had overwhelmed her, making her retreat into herself.

A man walked over and patted Jenna's shoulder. "God has a plan for your sister, and she's in all of our prayers. Don't lose hope."

Jenna nodded. Melanie sank a little lower in her chair.

Jesse stood up as the man walked away. "Jenna, I just wanted to see you, to say that I'm definitely here if you need anything. But you already have a lot of people around, so I'm going to go now and free up some room. Okay?"

"Okay," she murmured. "Thanks, Jesse."

"Me too," Melanie said impulsively. "But you can call me anytime. You have my number. And we'll all be checking every day to see how Sarah's doing."

Jenna nodded silently, her eyes down on Jesse's flowers. Melanie followed Jesse to the elevator, wishing she could have done more.

"How are you getting home?" he asked as the elevator descended. "For that matter, how did you get here?"

"Leah drove me, Miguel, and Ben, but they all left and I decided to stay." She shrugged. "There's always the bus."

Jesse leaned against the elevator wall. His brown hair had grown long enough to fall over his blue eyes again. He seemed to study her from behind a few strands.

"I could run you home if you want," he said slowly.

She looked for his old, self-satisfied smirk but found no trace of his former cockiness. He barely seemed to care which way she answered.

"All right. Thanks."

For the rest of the ride down to the lobby and all the way out to the car, neither one of them spoke. "That's tough about Sarah," Jesse said when they were finally on the road. "Jenna's taking it even harder than Peter said."

"Yeah. I don't know what's wrong with her. I mean, no one's saying this isn't awful. But the way she's acting, like she's already given up . . . it just doesn't seem like Jenna."

"Well, it couldn't have been easy seeing her sister get hit like that. Maybe she's still in shock."

"Maybe."

"I don't know what I'd do if that happened to Brittany," he said, taking a deep breath. His hands flexed unconsciously on the wheel. "You'd just want to kill the drunk who did it, wouldn't you?"

"*I* would, but I doubt murder has occurred to Jenna. It wouldn't be very Christian."

"Maybe not, but if it hasn't, she's a saint. What kind of idiot drinks and drives? If Sarah dies, that *will* be murder."

Given Jesse's own past problems with alcohol, Melanie found his outburst surprising. Numerous comments sprang to mind about idiots who drink.

"I don't know," she said at last, not wanting to start a fight.

He turned a corner, his eyes scanning the road ahead. "I quit drinking, you know," he said abruptly.

Melanie felt her brows go up. Did he mean he'd quit for now, for good, or for what? *When* had he quit?

"My stepsister, Bee, and I made a pact. Neither of us is drinking again until we're twenty-one."

"You made a pact with *Brittany*? Isn't she, like, twelve years old?"

Jesse made a face. "Drinking seems to run in my family. I mean, my extended family. Whatever." He shrugged his broad shoulders. "Brittany, well . . . she needed someone to set an example. And I'm going to do it."

Melanie sank back in the leather seat, amazed. "I didn't think you even *liked* her that much."

He shook his head impatiently. "I didn't know her. A lot of things have changed."

I'll say, Melanie thought.

"I mean, I was basically at that point anyway. Brittany running away last week just made up my mind a little faster."

"Brittany ran away?" she echoed, hopelessly lost.

"She needs *someone* to act like an adult. So the two us made an agreement. And now, with this accident . . . well, I'm doubly glad we did."

Every curve of Jesse's face was familiar. Every gesture, every expression . . .

And he seemed like a total stranger. Could he really have changed so much in just the month since they'd broken up?

"I guess—I guess Brittany really looks up to you now," Melanie stammered uncertainly.

He shrugged again as he pulled into her driveway. "I guess she always did."

The ride was over. Melanie reached to open the passenger door, everything inside her clamoring to invite him in.

"Do you . . . uh . . . do you think Sarah will get better?" she asked, chickening out at the last second. There was no way she was giving Jesse the chance to hurt her again.

She still wasn't over the last time.

"There she is." Nicole pointed ahead as she and Guy stepped off the elevator. "She's sitting with her sisters."

Guy moved forward with Nicole. "How many sisters does she have?" he asked, surprised.

"Um, five. There's six of them altogether. Six girls. Plus Mrs. Conrad. And Mr. Conrad, of course, but he's not a girl. Obviously."

She knew she was babbling, but she couldn't seem to stop. Ever since Guy had picked her up that afternoon, she'd been totally on edge. Was this a date? Were they just friends? And should she even be wondering things like that when they were on their way to visit someone in a coma?

There was no one in the waiting room except for the Conrad sisters. Nicole left Guy to rush to Jenna, who sat between an empty seat and Caitlin.

"How are you doing?" she asked, taking the vacant chair. "I've been so worried about you! How's Sarah?"

"I'm all right," Jenna answered unconvincingly. "Sarah's about the same. My parents are in there now."

"But if she's not getting worse, then that's good,

isn't it?" Nicole tried to sound encouraging. "We brought you some cookies," she added, dropping the stiff white bag in her friend's lap.

"Cookies?" Allison leaned forward from down the row.

"There's, uh, there's probably enough for everyone," said Nicole, wishing now she'd bought more than a dozen. She should have realized Jenna would have to share.

Jenna passed the bag to Caitlin, who handed it over to Allison.

"Hello, Jenna," said Guy, walking over to stand in front of them. "Remember me at all?"

Nicole jumped up, realizing too late that she had totally abandoned him. "Of course you know Guy," she told Jenna. "From Los Angeles. Remember?"

Jenna looked up, then rose slowly to her feet, her eyes fixed on Guy Vaughn. "What are you doing here?"

"Nicole called me. I just want to say that if there's anything I can do, anything at all . . . I have a younger sister too. I can only imagine what you're going through."

Jenna seemed almost starstruck as Guy held out his hand. She stared, then slowly put her palm against his. He squeezed it between both his own, as if trying to press his strength into her.

"Hello," another male voice said, breaking in on the moment. Nicole looked up to see Peter coming from the direction of the elevator, bags of chips and pretzels clutched in both hands. "I'm Peter Altmann."

"Guy Vaughn." Guy released Jenna's hand to shake with Peter, who dropped the snacks in Caitlin's lap.

"Not . . . not the singer from Los Angeles?" Peter said.

Guy glanced at Jenna, clearly surprised. "I didn't realize I'd made that big an impression."

Peter steered Jenna back toward her chair and motioned for Guy to take the seat beside her. "You guys opened for Fire & Water, right?"

"Is that right?" Maggie demanded, getting up to crowd in closer.

Allison followed her over. "You know Fire & Water?"

"I don't exactly *know* them," Guy said modestly. "I met them once, though. They're really cool."

The younger girls started firing off questions, while Peter used the distraction to whisper to Nicole. "Thanks for bringing him," he said gratefully. "Anything to cheer her up . . ."

Jenna didn't look particularly cheered to Nicole. She listened to the talk with some interest at first, but after a few minutes she seemed to drift away, lost in her own thoughts. Guy stood up, as if sensing the same thing.

"Here, Nicole," he said, gesturing for her to take his chair. "I know you want to talk to Jenna."

She *did* want to talk to Jenna. She just wished she could think of something good to say. "Everyone in Eight Prime is thinking about you," she tried lamely.

Jenna nodded. The bit of animation she'd shown on first seeing Guy had disappeared completely.

"I'll bet I'm thinking about you the most, though," Nicole added before she realized how conceited that sounded. "I mean, except for Peter, of course. And not that the others aren't *thinking* about you . . ."

She glanced back at the guys, desperate for some help. They shrugged and shook their heads, as stymied as Nicole.

If only I knew some magic words, she thought. *Something I could say that would make everything all right.*

But she didn't. Nobody did.

And then she had an idea. Glancing self-consciously around her, she leaned in closer to Jenna. "I'll, uh . . . I'll pray for Sarah," she whispered shyly. "Every morning and every night, until she's well again."

"Really?" Jenna's eyes caught a spark that hadn't been there before. "You're not just saying that?"

Nicole shook her head, embarrassed. "It's not the kind of thing I go around saying."

"Right." Jenna smiled, the first genuine smile Nicole had seen. "Thanks, Nicole."

Nicole could feel herself blushing, wondering if

everyone had heard. Not that anyone in her current company would probably think anything of it, but still . . .

She stood up abruptly, strangely near tears. "I'm going to go now. Peter's keeping us up to date on Sarah, and if you ever need me, well . . . call me," she urged in a husky voice, nearly running to the elevator.

What's the matter with you? she rebuked herself on the ride down to the lobby. She had known a visit to Intensive Care wasn't a trip to the mall—she should have been more prepared. Instead, she had totally fallen apart. She was too humiliated even to look at Guy, who rode silently beside her.

Out in the parking lot, though, she couldn't avoid facing him as he let her into his car. She met his eyes reluctantly, wondering what he must think of her. She was always so flighty around him, so incredibly immature.

But to her amazement, his expression seemed to say that she hadn't blown it at all. He searched her face with great seriousness, as if seeing her for the first time. Her heart beat a little faster, answering his gaze.

Then, slowly, Guy smiled.

"I made a huge mistake after our first date," he said ruefully. "I *really* want to see you again."

Peter's hand tightened over Jenna's as Mr. and Mrs. Conrad walked back into the waiting room beside one of Sarah's many doctors. There was no one left in the room except the Conrad girls and Peter, and they all stood up at once as the grim-looking trio approached.

Please don't let this be bad news, Peter prayed, feeling his stomach tighten. *Please, God, let Sarah live.*

"How is she, Dr. Malone?" Mary Beth asked immediately, her voice calm and steady. "Is she doing any better?"

The doctor glanced at Mr. and Mrs. Conrad, then regretfully shook his head. "I'm afraid things are a little worse."

"Worse!" Jenna wailed. "How could they be *worse?*"

Mrs. Conrad left her husband's side to put a reassuring arm around Jenna. "Your dad and I have asked Dr. Malone to explain things to you girls, but you're going to have to be quieter. There are other patients to think of."

Peter saw Jenna shudder with the effort of suppressing her emotions. "How could Sarah be worse?" she repeated in a quiet, shaky voice.

"Well, first the good news," the doctor hedged. "The orthopedic surgeon did a beautiful job on her leg. Her ribs seem to be mending fine too, and the splenectomy went well."

"So?" Jenna prompted anxiously.

"Any time you're dealing with coma, you have a

dangerous situation. I had really hoped she'd be back with us by now, but . . ." The doctor shook his head, as if trying to dispel his own bad news. "Of course, people have come out of much longer comas perfectly all right. But the longer things go on this way, the greater the chances of permanent damage."

"You mean *brain* damage?" Allison asked disbelievingly. "Sarah's going to be a vegetable?"

"He didn't say that," Mrs. Conrad put in quickly.

The doctor nodded. "It's too soon to know the future, and of course we still have hope. The next few days will be critical. After that, we'll have to see."

"You mean if she lives a few more days," Jenna accused bitterly. "Isn't that what you're really trying to say?"

"Jenna!" Mr. Conrad scolded.

But the doctor gave her a sympathetic look. "It could still go either way."

Jenna stared, then collapsed into tears, shrinking out of her mother's embrace to sit down on the floor. Peter crouched beside her and held her hand, heartbroken to see her so hurt, but she didn't even seem to realize he was there.

"He said it could go *either* way," Mary Beth said haughtily from above them. "Stop being so melodramatic."

Caitlin tried to whisper something, but Mary Beth waved her away.

"No! All day she's been acting like she's the only one losing a sister, and I'm sick of it. We're all hurting the same, Jenna."

Mary Beth's choice of words couldn't have been worse. At the mention of losing a sister, Jenna began to cry even more inconsolably, and Allison and Maggie joined in. Mrs. Conrad pressed her hands to her graying temples, as if her head might explode. Mr. Conrad walked the doctor partway to the elevator, then hurried back to his family.

"We're all of us in God's hands," he said, pulling Maggie and Allison into his arms. "And that hasn't changed a bit. It's just that right now we're all a little more aware of Sarah's presence there."

"That's right," Caitlin whispered. "We can't lose hope."

Mary Beth hung her head, as if sorry for the fuss she'd created, while Caitlin hugged her mother. The tears in the room died down as quickly as they had begun.

All except for Jenna's.

Tugging her hand loose from Peter's, she sobbed on by herself, rocking back and forth on the cold linoleum. He hovered beside her, desperate to be of some comfort, but he didn't know whether to hold her, say something, or just let her cry herself out. Mr. Conrad made the decision for him, walking over to touch him on the shoulder.

"She's just so tired she doesn't know what she's

doing. Why don't you go home now, Peter, and let us take care of her?"

"All right," Peter said reluctantly, forcing himself to his feet. The last thing he wanted was to leave, but maybe the family needed some time alone. "I'll call you later, Jenna. And I'll see you tomorrow at church. If you want, we can sit together."

She didn't reply. And now Mr. and Mrs. Conrad were both looking at him expectantly.

"Bye," he added, brushing his hand across the top of her bent head.

He walked slowly to the elevator, hoping Jenna still might realize he was leaving and have some parting words.

She never even looked up.

Six

Jenna sat in the pew with her family on Sunday, her heart too heavy to sing with the choir. Her mother wasn't up front with them that day, either, having turned her directing duties over to Mrs. Jackson so that she could stay at the hospital with Sarah.

I don't know why it's okay for her and not me. Jenna had begged to go to the hospital too, but her parents had insisted on her going to church instead. Now she stared at her lap instead of joining in the hymn, completely unable to get in the spirit.

"Why aren't you singing?" Peter leaned over to whisper. "It might make you feel better."

Jenna didn't even look at him. Nothing was going to make her feel better, especially not having him stick to her like glue, pretending nothing was wrong between them. *I'd set him straight in a hurry if I didn't have more important things to worry about.*

But she knew she was probably fooling herself. She had no idea what to do about the situation with Peter, and if she didn't exactly encourage him to sit beside her and hold her hand, she didn't tell him not to, either. Maybe letting Peter force attention on her wasn't much of a relationship, but it was the only one they had at the moment.

"Let us pray," Reverend Thompson said, beginning the service.

Jenna tried to pray, but her words came out all jumbled. Usually she thanked God for her blessings: her mother, father, and sisters, and their safe, happy life together. She didn't know what to say to him now. She struggled along, barely going through the motions, until the congregation began a special prayer for Sarah's recovery.

For a moment, her heart rose up, almost reassured, almost able to connect . . . She caught her breath in anticipation.

And then she lost it again.

What good was being in church when her heart and soul were back at the hospital with Sarah?

Boy, this is familiar, thought Miguel, walking through the hospital lobby on his own after mass.

Visiting with Leah the day before had prepared him for the flood of memories washing over him now, but that didn't make them less intense. Every sound, every smell, even the color of the walls, reminded him of the long days and nights he'd spent walking the halls around the time of his mother's kidney transplant. All night Saturday he'd barely been able to sleep, consumed with thoughts of the hospital, and the moment mass had ended that Sunday morning he'd made his excuses to his mother and come straight back.

What haunted him most was the memory of how motivated he'd been after his mother's surgery to become a doctor himself. He had even thought at the time that he'd actually made up his mind to do it. But now, months later, he still hadn't so much as looked into what achieving that dream would involve. He felt like he'd let himself down, but there were just so many other things already on his plate: Leah leaving, his job with Sabrina, improving his living situation, Eight Prime, the impending water polo season . . .

I can only do so many things at once, he thought, sighing as he punched the elevator button.

Upstairs, the waiting room for the intensive care unit was totally empty—not even one Conrad in sight. Miguel started to cross to the nurses' station, then changed his mind and direction, wandering down the short hall leading to the bathrooms instead.

They must all still be at church, he thought, peering out a small square window at the parking lot below. *I might as well hang around a few minutes and see if Jenna shows up.*

He didn't know what comfort he could give that hadn't been offered the day before, but something strong had drawn him there that morning. Maybe he'd find out what if he waited for the Conrads.

Turning away from the window, Miguel walked slowly back down the hall toward the waiting room. A bulletin board caught his eye, and he stopped to read the announcements. There wasn't much there—a few cards from former patients, a cafeteria menu, a crayon rendering of a rainbow. He was already starting to move on when a typed notice in the corner grabbed his attention.

Volunteers Wanted—All Ages

The Clearwater Crossing Children's Auxiliary encourages volunteers of all ages to contact us. There is always a need for cheerful faces to visit the children's ward to play games, read stories, and otherwise entertain the youngsters here for long stays. An hour of your time can make all the difference to a sick or lonely child.

Won't you help? Call 555-1919.

Miguel froze, everything else forgotten as he read the notice again. *What an awesome thing to do!* he thought.

He could easily see himself volunteering, toting

his checker and chess sets from home, along with his favorite old mystery novels. If enough kids wanted to listen, he could read them a chapter a day—always making sure to end in some particularly suspenseful place.

Miguel! he imagined them protesting. *You can't just leave us hanging without telling us what happens!*

But he wouldn't tell. He'd make them wait until the next day, when he'd show up to find them already gathered for the next installment, too curious about the story to dwell on being sick. He smiled at the thought of the boisterous way they would greet him, and for a long, sweet moment, it all seemed possible.

Then reality checked in.

Oh, who are you kidding? he asked himself. *How can you volunteer at the hospital on top of everything else you're supposed to be doing?*

He stood there another moment, looking longingly at the notice.

You can't, he decided sadly.

It's the prettiest necklace I've ever seen—a blood-red garnet cut in the shape of a heart. When we walk tomorrow for graduation, Trent wants me to wear it outside my gown. Then, when I get to the stage, I'm supposed to point to it as a signal to him and everyone else that the two of us are

*together. We don't know where he'll be when I'm
onstage, though, or if he'll even be able to see me.
My parents, on the other hand, will be right up
front and center, and they already think this thing
with Trent is moving way too fast. Calling attention to ourselves at graduation would be all the
proof they need.*

*On the other hand, lots of other couples are do-
ing stuff. It's not like we'd be the only ones. Katie
Jensen and Mike Madson are supposedly wearing
matching T-shirts that say <u>Katie + Mike Forever,</u>
and when they get onstage they're going to unzip
their gowns and flash them at everyone. Personally, I think that's a little much, but my point is that
after something like that Trent and I would look
dignified, relatively speaking.*

Melanie smiled as she turned the page, totally absorbed in her mother's high-school life. Her father
had already been asleep for hours that Monday
night, leaving her safe to read in bed without fear of
interruption. She was now completely engrossed by
the growing bond between Tristyn and Trent, one
that had deepened and strengthened immensely, despite her dire early predictions.

*If only my parents weren't so overprotective!
They liked Trent fine at first, but now that it's*

serious they're acting totally different. I know we'll have a battle about curfew tomorrow night. Between midnight bowling for Grad Night and all the private parties, practically everyone I know is staying out all night. So why shouldn't I? I'm eighteen now, and they ought to admit it instead of treating me like a child. If I have to, I guess I'll break curfew. I'd rather have a fight the next morning than spend my whole life wondering what I missed.

I wonder what Trent's doing right now? He's probably asleep. I wish I could sneak into his bedroom and wake him up. Wouldn't he be surprised! A lot of people would be, probably, but I just love him so much, it's like he's all I can think about. It's weird now to think how much we fought when we first started dating, because now it's like there were never any doubts. We're completely past all that. I never thought I'd get to the point where a guy I was with could tell a stupid joke or wear a completely embarrassing shirt and I wouldn't even care. When Trent and I got together, I was the first one to notice that stuff. I was judging him all the time. But now . . . I mean, other people have to point those things out to me. It's like something's come over us and we've moved to this whole different

The phone rang in the silent house, startling Melanie halfway out of bed. She jumped up, throwing the diary to one side and trying to untangle herself from the blankets before it rang again. All she needed was for her father to wake up.

"Hello!" she said, fumbling with the talk button on her cordless.

"Melanie?"

"Peter?"

For a moment she was curious. Peter never called her anymore, especially not so late at night. Then she felt nearly ill. "Is it Sarah? Has something bad happened?"

"No. Sarah's the same." Peter sounded exhausted, and Melanie realized he had probably just gotten home from another long stint at the hospital. "The reason I'm calling is that Jenna's coming back to school tomorrow, and I want Eight Prime to eat together in the cafeteria. Just to welcome her back, you know? Ben's going to get us a table."

"All right. Are we doing anything special?"

"No. It's just that she really doesn't want to come back. She wants to stay at the hospital until Sarah's out of danger, but her parents think she needs to return to a normal life—as normal as possible, anyway. No one knows how long Sarah might be comatose, and Jenna can't miss school forever."

"She's only been out a couple of days," Melanie said slowly, trying to remember. "Friday and Monday, right? That's not such a big deal. I missed a lot more when I hurt my head."

Peter sighed. "It's not just the school she's missing. It's the way she's acting. Everyone's upset. Everyone's concerned. But Jenna—it's like she holds herself personally responsible or something."

"That's ridiculous."

"Of course it is. Maybe because she was there to see it happen . . . No one really understands why. Anyway, her parents want her to cheer up, so they're sending her back to school."

Melanie couldn't suppress a snicker. "Oh, yeah. That ought to do it."

He sighed again. "Jenna is *not* happy about it."

"Well, I'll be there for lunch, and I'll do my best to be cheery. If she's not less depressed than on Saturday, though, I'm afraid it won't do much good."

"Thanks, Melanie. She may not show it right now, but I know having her friends support her really means a lot."

Melanie hung up the phone, wondering if Peter was right. *He's right about one thing: Jenna's a mess.* For that matter, Peter was starting to sound like he was barely hanging in there.

Sarah's accident was a terrible thing, but Melanie had always assumed that disasters were somehow easier for people who believed in God. While everyone else was scrambling, trying to come up with an answer, they already had one. When Kurt Englbehrt had died, for instance, Peter and Jenna had seemed far better able to deal with it than most of the other students. This time, however . . . this time they weren't doing nearly so well.

This time it's personal, Melanie thought with a touch of irony.

Was it possible her Christian friends were having trouble practicing what they preached?

Seven

"Wait until you see what I brought for dessert," Peter told the group assembled in the cafeteria. "Homemade chocolate chip *and* peanut butter cookies. My mom's been baking overtime."

Taking the bag of cookies carefully from his backpack, he set it proudly on the table in front of Jenna. It had been no easy trick carrying cookies around all morning without smashing them to crumbs, but it would be worth all the trouble if Jenna only smiled.

"Dessert!" Nicole said disapprovingly. "We've barely started lunch."

"I can eat both at the same time," Ben said hopefully, his eyes glued to the bag.

Peter thought of making everyone wait until Jenna had finished her meal, but the way she was picking at her food, that could take a while. Pulling the bag back toward him, he took out four of the biggest, most perfect cookies before he passed it to Ben.

"Don't you like your pizza?" Peter asked quietly,

balancing the cookies on the edge of Jenna's tray. "I thought you usually liked that."

"It's okay." Jenna stabbed at her salad instead. "I wanted to bring my lunch, but nobody's been to the grocery store."

"I'm not surprised," Leah said sympathetically. "You've all had a few other things on your minds."

"What's the latest on Sarah?" Melanie asked. "Is she doing any better?"

Peter cringed. He had hoped to fill everyone in before lunch, so that no one asked Jenna that question. With everything else he'd had to do, though, he hadn't found Melanie in time.

Jenna shook her head, her eyes on her tray. "She's still in a coma. The doctors have a lot of theories, and that's about it."

"Hey, I could take you to the store after school, if you want," Jesse offered. "I take Charlie all the time—I'm practically a pro."

"Thanks, but my dad is going today."

"I stopped by the hospital Sunday morning," said Miguel, "but I missed you guys somehow. You must have still been at church."

"Probably."

Peter smiled encouragingly, but even to him the expression felt desperate. He was thrilled to have Jenna at school again, and all her friends had shown up, trying to make her feel better. But none of that seemed to matter. Instead of putting on the brave

91

face he now realized he'd come to expect from her, Jenna made no effort to hide her pain. Rather than using the opportunity to speak of hope, she let every feature show her despair. She wasn't even eating her cookies.

The Jenna he knew would never act this way.

"The, uh, the last basketball game is this Friday," Nicole offered, obviously straining to make conversation. "The last one before districts, that is."

"We aren't going to districts." Jesse seemed to take a certain satisfaction in the fact. "Not with our record."

"It's just as well." Melanie pushed the rest of her lunch aside and selected a peanut butter cookie from the bag going around the table. "I've had about all the cheering I can take."

"Until next year, you mean," said Nicole, waving the bag away.

"Maybe."

"It's not completely over, is it?" Leah asked. "Don't you guys cheer for the track team, and water polo, and all the other sports?"

Melanie shrugged. "Not too much. Only when they expect a crowd. Otherwise, what are we doing there?"

"Supporting the teams?" Jesse suggested sarcastically.

"Like they care." Melanie turned to Miguel. "Can you guys even hear us when you're underwater?"

Miguel laughed. "We're not usually *under*water. Not on a good day, anyway."

"The track team could hear you," Ben pointed out, helping himself to a second handful of cookies. "You guys could stand up in the bleachers and yell."

Melanie gave him an incredulous look before turning her attention back to the group. "I'll just be glad to spend as little time with Vanessa and Tiffany as possible," she said, naming the senior squad leader and another senior girl. "Those two give me a shooting pain right between the eyes."

Nicole giggled, then quickly stifled herself. "Are they going to be judges for cheer tryouts in April?"

"I don't know. Normally they would be, but with Sandra running things now, I won't be surprised if it's all different. Maybe she'll do it herself."

Peter kept one ear on the conversation as it moved from cheerleading to baseball to the recent cold snap, but his eyes never left Jenna. She toyed with her fork, twisting it around and around in her salad as though the lettuce were spaghetti. She pulled the cheese off her pizza. Finally, she gnawed the edge of a cookie, not even seeming to notice that he'd brought her two favorites. She was with the group in body, but anyone could see that her spirit was far away.

The end-of-lunch bell was a relief for everyone.

"Well! Off to class!" Melanie said, rising along with the rest of the group. "I'll see you guys later.

Jenna . . ." She hesitated, clearly wanting to say something uplifting. "We're all keeping a good thought for your sister."

The others murmured similar things as they scattered for their classes, leaving Peter and Jenna alone.

"I'll just wrap these up," Peter said, trying not to show his disappointment as he put the three cookies Jenna hadn't touched into the bag with the few that were left. "You can put this in your backpack for when you get hungry later."

Jenna shook her head, and now there were tears in her eyes. "I feel like I'll never be hungry again."

He put his arm around her, ignoring the fact that the cafeteria was emptying and they'd probably be late for class. "I wish I could do something for you, Jenna. It kills me to see you so down."

"You've done enough."

"I've done everything I can think of, but I feel like . . . I don't know. You can't just give up, Jenna. You have to have faith." Lifting the cross dangling from her neck, he closed one of her hands around it. "This isn't over yet. And don't forget that your friends are here for you. *I'm* here for you."

She held the cross a moment, then let it drop back to her chest. "Thanks, but right now that sounds pretty hollow. I have to go to class." A tear spilled onto her cheek as she shouldered her backpack and hurried away.

Peter watched her go with tears in his eyes too. "What is *wrong* with me?" he moaned, dropping his head to the table.

Jenna was his girlfriend, his best friend, the love of his life . . . shouldn't he be able to help her through a crisis? All he wanted was to support her, to comfort her, to reassure her that all wasn't lost. And everything inside him insisted he ought to be able to handle the job.

So why do I keep failing?

The whole time he'd known Jenna, she had never needed him more.

And I have never been less help.

"I don't know, Courtney," Nicole said worriedly. "If you had just seen her at lunch today . . ."

"Please! No more Jenna stories. I can't take it," Courtney declared, reaching across Nicole's bed for another magazine. "I wouldn't have come over if I'd known we were going to talk about the God Squad all night."

"Not all night," Nicole protested.

Courtney flipped through unseen pages. "I'm tired of hearing about it, all right? If Jenna and God are such good buddies, why doesn't she just call him up and tell him he's blowing it? Why does it have to involve me?"

Nicole bit back a rude answer. She knew Courtney wasn't really as cold as she sounded; she just didn't like to think about things she didn't know how to fix. Life was easier for her that way. And since it had been a long time since her best friend had dropped by, Nicole didn't want to push.

"I have a date this Saturday," she said instead, changing the subject.

"No way!" Courtney abandoned her magazine, eyes alight. Swinging her legs to the floor, she perched on the edge of the bed and leaned forward toward Nicole. "Who are you going out with?"

"It's someone you know," said Nicole, rolling her desk chair back a couple of inches. "You have to guess."

"Someone *I* know?" Courtney clearly found the current discussion more to her liking than talk of accidents and hospitals. "Who could it be? Not Jesse!"

"*Not* Jesse," Nicole confirmed, surprised Courtney would even guess him after everything that had happened.

"Let's see," Courtney mused. "Miguel's still with Leah, and Peter's with Jenna, so . . . Ben Pipkin!" she guessed next.

Nicole almost fell off her chair. "Are you *kidding* me?"

She and Courtney had had their differences, but naming Ben was just plain insulting. Courtney laughed.

"It's Guy Vaughn," said Nicole, anxious to head off further guesses.

"But—I—I thought you hated him!" Courtney sputtered. "I thought he hated *you*!"

"Granted, we didn't hit it off too well at first. But—"

"I'll say you didn't! It felt like nuclear winter in the backseat of that car."

"But I've seen him a few times since then, and now—"

"When? When have you seen him?" Courtney demanded. "Just at that Bible thing."

"That was one place," Nicole said slowly, reminded again how much distance had crept between her and her best friend. "Then I saw him again in L.A. He was there for that rally and we were staying in the same hotel. And since we've gotten back, I've run into him a couple more times . . ."

She decided against mentioning their recent trip to the hospital, as that would only take her back to the forbidden topic of Jenna.

"I can't believe it! I *told* you you two were perfect for each other!"

"No, you told me he was a religious freak, and you begged me to go out with him."

"Whatever." Courtney shook her head, the grin on her face enormous. "You and Guy. I can't believe it."

"Yeah, well. I'm kind of surprised myself."

"But this is fantastic!" Courtney exclaimed. "I couldn't have planned this better."

"Huh?"

"Don't be dense, Nicole. You're back with Guy, and I want to get back with his good friend Jeff."

"I'm not exactly *with* him," Nicole corrected dubiously.

"Stop making things harder than they are. Don't you see how perfect this is?"

"It's just one date."

"No! This is the perfect chance to dig for information about Jeff. You could find out all kinds of things, if you'd just ask the right questions."

"Like what?" Nicole was already pretty sure she didn't want to know.

"Like whether Jeff has seen anyone since he and I broke up. If so, who? Find out whether he talks about me, and what he says."

"You want me to ask Guy *that?*"

"No!" Courtney took a deep breath and pushed her red hair back with both hands. "You don't come right out and *ask*, Nicole. You work it into the conversation. Casually."

"Oh." Working Courtney into a conversation with Guy, casually or not, wasn't something Nicole cared to try. It wasn't as if Guy and Courtney had anything in common, so he was almost sure to catch on to Nicole's hidden agenda. Even if he didn't, she'd be scared he was going to the whole evening. "I'm not sure that's such a good idea."

"Don't be silly." Courtney fell backward onto the bed, clearly delighted with her plan.

But when Nicole didn't reply, she sat back up again, the smile gone from her face. "It's not like I ask for so much, Nicole."

And then the coup de grâce: "Emily would do it."

"I never said I wouldn't," Nicole retorted, knowing she had to now. "*If* you're sure that's what you want."

"It is."

"All right, then. Fine."

Nicole picked up a magazine and stared blindly at the cover. *I must be crazy to have agreed to such a stupid idea!*

On the other hand, here, finally, was something she could do for Courtney that Emily couldn't. And if she was ever going to get rid of that girl, she needed to grab every advantage.

Nicole shook her head to clear her doubts, refusing to hear the ones that still lingered.

Why am I even worrying? I already said I'd do it. Done deal.

"I'm locking the car," said Leah. "In case you want to leave anything here."

"I'm leaving my backpack," Melanie said, tossing it into the backseat. "No point lugging it all over the hospital."

Nicole decided to leave hers, too, and Leah locked the doors. "I hope Jenna's here," she said as they crossed the parking lot.

The girls had only made the decision to visit during lunchtime that Wednesday. Jenna and Peter had been in the cafeteria but holed up in a corner, and it hadn't felt right to butt in. Jenna had still looked so haunted, though, they'd felt like they had to do something. Melanie was the one who had proposed a trip to the hospital after school, but as the three of them walked toward the lobby she hoped that had been a good plan. Maybe all Jenna *really* wanted was to be alone.

That's what I'd want, Melanie realized. *Or just with my family—if I had a family like Jenna's.*

They got into the elevator, Melanie still having second thoughts. "Maybe we shouldn't have come," she said.

"What?" said Leah.

"Why not?" Nicole demanded.

"Maybe Jenna doesn't want us here. I mean, she never said she did, right? That was Peter's idea."

Leah looked thoughtful, but Nicole made a face.

"Don't be ridiculous. Of course she wants us. We're her *friends*. Besides, you're the one who said we should."

The elevator doors opened on the fifth floor. "We're here now," Leah said, making further discussion pointless.

Jenna wasn't in the waiting room, though. None of the Conrads were.

"This is weird," Leah said slowly. "I'd have sworn she'd be here by now. We gave her a good head start."

"*Some*body ought to be here," Melanie said.

Nicole walked up to the nurses' station. "Isn't any of Sarah Conrad's family here?"

"Yes. We transferred Sarah to a private room today," the nurse told them. "If you're quiet and don't stay long, I can let you see her."

"Really?" said Melanie, surprised. Actually seeing Sarah was the last thing she had expected. Except for random encounters during an Eight Prime meeting at Jenna's house, none of them even knew Sarah.

"It's the last door on the left," said the nurse, leaning out over the desk to point down a side passage. "One of her sisters is already in there."

"I'll bet it's Jenna," Leah said with obvious relief. "Come on."

But Melanie lagged behind. "If you moved her to her own room, that must mean she's doing better. Right?"

The nurse shifted her weight uncomfortably, a play of emotions on her face. "It means we had a room. Now, I'm not kidding. You girls act like adults in there, or I won't let you visit again."

The trio crept down the hallway, afraid even of walking loudly after the nurse's warning. The rooms they passed on the way had windows facing the hall as well as windows in the doors. Some had the blinds drawn for privacy, some gave the girls a clear view of the people inside, hooked to various machines.

"How awful," whispered Nicole. "This is even worse than I thought."

Melanie walked in silence, her thoughts on her own hospitalization after her head injury. At the time, everyone had thought that was pretty serious. Now she knew how lucky she'd been. The part of the hospital she'd stayed in was nowhere near as scary as this.

"This is it," said Leah, peeking between the partially open blinds on the last window. "I see Jenna."

With the lightest possible knock, Leah pushed the door open. Jenna looked toward them, startled, then tried to force a smile. Her face was wet with tears, though, and she looked so pitiful sitting there that Melanie's heart turned over.

"Where's Peter?" she asked, hurrying forward. "You're not here all alone?"

"No." Jenna nodded toward the bed.

Melanie stopped and looked. "That's Sarah?" she whispered, stunned.

She had retained a vague mental picture of Jenna's youngest sister—ten years old, blond, pixie chin— but the girl in the bed looked so small and helpless it took her breath away. Except for the bruises, Sarah's face was as pale as her pillow. Her blond hair fanned around her head as if someone had combed it that way. A ventilator did her breathing, her slight chest rising and falling to someone else's rhythm. Tubes, IVs, and monitors cluttered the sterile bedside, some entering Sarah's body in plain view, others disappearing beneath the thin blanket.

She's dying. One look and Melanie had never been more certain of anything. *No wonder Jenna has given up hope.*

Melanie moved slowly to the bedside, the rest of the room disappearing as she focused on the injured girl. It had been easy to keep her fear and concern at a distance when she hadn't seen Sarah, when Sarah's dying had been hypothetical. Now, suddenly, all she could think about was the car accident that had killed her mother . . . and the one that had taken Kurt . . . Would Sarah be next?

Instinctively she took the girl's hand and squeezed it. "Hang on, Sarah," she whispered intensely. "Don't you die on us."

Sarah didn't move even an eyelid. Her monitors showed no change.

But a ragged sob broke the silence. Melanie turned to see Leah slip into the chair beside Jenna's, folding their crying friend into a fiercely protective hug.

"No one knows the future," Leah said softly. "For all we know, Sarah can hear us right now."

Jenna's sobs abated a little, then broke out again

in full force. Melanie and Nicole exchanged helpless glances.

"I'm scared, Leah," Jenna sobbed into the older girl's shoulder. "I'm trying not to be, but I just . . . just . . ."

The tears took over, choking out her voice. Leah held her tightly, waiting silently.

"Oh, God," Jenna finally got out. "You have no idea how scared I am."

Eight

"Are you going to eat that hamburger, or reheat it with your X-ray vision?" Leah teased, tossing a french fry across the table at Miguel. "We have to get back to school today, you know."

"I'm thinking!" Miguel protested. Picking the fry up off the tray where it had landed, he put it in his mouth.

"Well, could you think a little louder? I'd get more conversation from a cactus."

"Ha, ha. Very funny." Miguel took a bite of his hamburger, already lost in space again.

Leah looked around the crowded restaurant and sighed. A sudden warming of the weather had sent CCHS students off campus in droves that Thursday, if only long enough for lunch. Leah had begged Miguel to take her to Burger City—just the two of them—but she might as well have gone by herself. At every stool and table, groups of buddies laughed as they ate, or couples talked in lowered voices, their heads bent close together. At every table but Leah's, that was. Miguel had been somewhere else since they'd walked in.

"What are you thinking *about?*" Leah asked, trying one last time. "Tell me quick and I'll give you the rest of my fries."

"The hospital," he answered, hand extended for the bag.

Leah nodded as she made good on her promise. "I should have known. You mean Sarah."

"Uh, no," he said, a little guiltily. "Not really."

"What then?"

"When I stopped by there on Sunday, I saw this notice for volunteers to help in the children's ward. I can't do it. But it's been bugging me ever since."

"Because you want to?" she guessed.

"Because I *really* want to." Miguel's brown eyes were intense. "I'd be helping kids, plus it would be a good chance to get a feel for how a hospital works and what being a doctor's like. But how can I volunteer with everything else I've got going on? If only . . . well, I just wish I weren't working so many hours."

You and me both! Leah thought. If Miguel wanted to volunteer at the hospital, that seemed like a worthy cause to her. But the truth was she'd rather see him do nearly anything than spend so much time with Sabrina. Every time she dared to suggest he cut back his hours, though, he swore it was impossible.

"Maybe you could cut back your hours," she suggested anyway.

Miguel made the usual pained face. "No."

"Or, wait! I know! Maybe instead of volunteering you could get a *job* at the hospital. One that pays."

He shook his head. "Doing what? Washing dishes in the cafeteria?"

"Well, they aren't going to put you in surgery," she said impatiently. "But think about it, Miguel. If you were already working there doing something else, you could probably squeeze in an extra hour with the kids pretty easily. And you don't know what kinds of jobs they have until you ask."

"I'm not trained for anything I'd want to do," he said, dragging the final french fry around in a puddle of ketchup. "Any job they had for me would be at minimum wage."

"You have to start somewhere."

Dropping the fry, he gave her an amazed look. "I've already started somewhere, Leah. Mr. Ambrosi pays me good money. What *you're* saying is I should start over."

"Um, yes," she admitted. "I guess so. But if you're really going to be a doctor, you'll have to start over sometime. And the longer you wait, the worse making that change will look. Why not do it now, while you're only working part-time?"

"Because." Pushing his tray away, he rose abruptly to his feet. "You ready? We've got to get going."

"I'm ready," she said sweetly, following him to the door.

Once they would have had a fight. Once Leah would have tossed all night, wondering what he was thinking. Now she walked quietly out to his car, content that she already knew.

He was considering her idea.

Please let them have something good, she thought, crossing her fingers. *Something he likes that gets him away from Sabrina.*

Having Miguel work at the hospital was the perfect way to make *two* people happy.

I wish Mom and Dad would just get off my case!

Tristyn's loopy writing was larger than usual where that sentence scrawled the width of the page. Melanie smiled and bent lower over her desk, preparing to read for an hour or two before dinner. If her father happened to walk in, she could always cover the diary with some other book and say she was studying.

I am studying, she reminded herself. *I'm studying ancient history.*

It didn't feel that way, though, when nearly every word her mother wrote sounded like something any teenager might say. Eager to pick up the story again, she returned her attention to the diary.

Mom is making a career out of trying to run my life now, wanting to know where I'm going and what I'm doing every second. It's summer and I'm eighteen! Can't everyone just relax? I only have these last few months before I go away to college in New York, and Trent will be leaving too—in a totally different direction. I don't even want to think about fall. I just want to see him as much as I can, to spend every minute together. I don't know why my parents can't understand that. Instead they're constantly complaining about how they never see me, and how our last summer together should be special. They see me every day! And unless someone is dying and hasn't told me, I don't think this is our last summer, either. I think it's really selfish of them to expect me to hang around the house when they know I'd rather be with Trent. He's the one I might not have much more time with. Anything could happen when we go away to college.

But I don't want to think about that. It's only June, and already I can't imagine what it will be like to say good-bye. I don't want to imagine it. Me and Trent, I don't know. It's like we were made for each other. Dad says I barely know him—that it's impossible to know anyone in such a short time—but I'm starting to think they'd say just about anything to keep me away from him. You should hear the questions they ask me. They're totally paranoid that we're having sex. If they came right out and asked me, maybe I would tell them. But why should I when the question is always something like

like the Bible Melanie had found hidden among her mom's painting supplies, and the fact that Aunt Gwen seemed to take church attendance for granted.

Melanie turned another page.

Trent was so romantic tonight! A bunch of us went up to the swimming hole, and I thought the mosquitoes were going to be awful, but they weren't. The air was so warm, and all the stars were out. We just spread a blanket under the big tree and sat around, plunking rocks down into the pond. It was like no one even wanted to talk, like a magic spell, and the fireflies . . . I don't know. I just know I'll never forget it. Like I'll be able to close my eyes when I'm thirty, or a hundred, and still hear the frogs down in the reeds and smell Trent's skin, warm, like soap and summer.

After a while, everyone else took off to do different things. Everyone but me and Trent. Mom and Dad would have called out the National Guard if they'd known we were up there alone, lying on a blanket, but it wasn't that way at all. We were just talking. Talking about everything we could think of, and that's when he said it.

I said, "How can you look around on a night like this and tell me you don't believe in God?" And he said, "God might be a stretch. But I think I see an angel right here."

Isn't that the most romantic thing ever? And then he kissed me. I almost died. I could have, easily. If we were allowed to pick our time, I can't imagine a more perfect moment than that. Just me and Trent on that blanket, our arms around each other, our eyes

The doorbell rang, jolting Melanie to her feet, heart pounding.

"Perfect timing," she complained, slamming the diary into a drawer. "Who's that?"

She wasn't expecting anyone. Her father *never* expected anyone. Running out of her bedroom, she trotted down the long curving staircase to the front door, her head still full of a perfect summer night and a guy with a clue what to say.

If only I'd meet someone like that, she thought wistfully, reaching for the doorknob. *I never meet anyone except for—*

"Jesse!" she exclaimed, stunned to find him standing on her doorstep. "I—I didn't expect it to be you."

"No," he agreed with an ironic smile.

He was wearing faded jeans and a leather jacket, his damp hair pushed back on his forehead. For a moment as he slouched in her doorway it was as if nothing had changed between them, as if he were there to pick her up for a date. Melanie's heart tugged painfully with the wish.

112

Because, of course, everything had changed between them.

"What are you doing here?" she asked before she stopped to think of something more polite. "I mean, uh, do you want to come in?"

He shook his head. "I'm on my way to the hospital, actually, to take a book to Jenna. I don't know if she'll like it, but . . ." He shrugged. "Want to go?"

"To the hospital? I was just there yesterday. All us girls went."

"Oh," he said, rebuffed. "Well, your house wasn't that far out of my way. I thought maybe you—"

"Would want to go again. I do, actually," she finished for him, grabbing her coat from the nearby closet. If Jesse could be an adult, so could she. "It was nice of you to think of me."

All right. That last comment might have been a little too much, she admitted as he looked her over with one cocked brow. It had always been a tricky thing, finding a balance with Jesse.

"So, should we go?" he asked.

"I'm ready."

She followed him through the gathering dusk to his car, her mind buzzing with questions. Had he finally forgiven her? Was that what his sudden appearance meant? Or was he really only thinking of the facts that she was too young to drive, and that Jenna might like to see her?

Maybe he's just embarrassed to go by himself, she thought, climbing in the passenger side. *Wait. No. He showed up alone last time.*

The most likely explanation was simple consideration. It just seemed so hard to believe, though, when there was so much history between them.

Rise above it, she thought as Jesse backed onto the road. *This isn't anything but two friends trying to do the right thing by another friend who needs them.*

She supposed she and Jesse were friends, anyway. They certainly weren't a couple.

"Do you think she hears a word we say?" Jenna turned in her chair to ask Caitlin. "I feel like I'm talking to the walls."

Caitlin chewed her lower lip. "I don't see how talking to her can *hurt*," she finally answered. "And maybe it does some good. You never know. We'll just have to wait for Sarah to tell us when she wakes up."

If she wakes up, Jenna thought, staring at her youngest sister through a haze of tears. It seemed the ache behind her eye sockets had become permanent, and if she'd once thought tears eventually had to run dry, now she suspected they fed on one another, creating an unlimited supply.

"I can't believe it's been a week," Jenna said. "In a way it seems like it just happened. Then a second later, it seems like our whole lives."

"It's the waiting," said Caitlin, fidgeting with the embroidery in her lap. "The not knowing . . ."

Jenna sighed. Sarah lay on the bed before them, seemingly completely unaware of their presence. She was still on the ventilator, its rhythmic whoosh loud in the quiet room. Sequential films of her brain and broken bones crowded the light boxes on the walls, dark in the absence of doctors. And if some of her bruises were starting to fade, there were new ones forming around the IVs on the backs of her hands, shockingly dark against skin that seemed more translucent every day.

"It was nice of Melanie and Jesse to stop by. All your friends have been nice."

"I guess." Jenna could have done without Melanie's visits, actually, but she didn't want to tell Caitlin why. Not now. Not when she was trying to forget the reason herself. It was bad enough seeing Peter, who continued to stick to her night and day like he had never done anything wrong.

At least she had convinced him not to come to the hospital that night, saying she wanted to spend time with Caitlin. As Sarah's stay in the hospital dragged on, the older members of the family had fallen into sitting with her in shifts, Jenna taking the one after school and Caitlin the one after dinner, before their father relieved them for the night. There was no reason Jenna couldn't stay through Caitlin's shift too, though. If her parents were more reasonable, she'd still be sleeping there.

"Well, I think you're lucky to have so many friends," Caitlin said. "I wish . . . Never mind."

But Jenna knew what her sister meant. "Cat, the only reason I have more friends than you do is because I'm not shy. If you ever let people see what you were really like, you'd have a million more friends than I do."

"No, I wouldn't," Caitlin mumbled, turning red.

"David figured it out, didn't he?" Jenna pushed restlessly out of her chair and bent low over her youngest sister. "Sarah? Sarah, can you hear me?" She watched in vain for a flicker of movement, for any indication that her words were getting through.

"Sarah, if you wake up, I'll make a batch of those seven-layer cookie bars you like and you can eat the whole panful. With a gallon of ice-cold milk. Wouldn't that be good? Wake up, and I'll go make them."

Nothing.

"You might get an argument from Mom on that one anyway," Caitlin said softly from behind her. "I doubt the first thing they want her eating is an entire pan of cookies."

"Don't listen, Sarah," Jenna urged. "I'll bet Mom'll let you have anything you want. Are you kidding? *Two* pans of cookies. But you have to wake up."

Nothing.

"Can't you hear me at all?" Jenna asked wistfully.

Caitlin rose to join her, stroking Sarah's arm through the blanket. "When you feel better, you can come walk dogs with us. Anytime you want," she offered, trying Jenna's strategy.

"Yes, and I'll let you borrow my CDs, and my books, and . . ." Jenna cast around desperately for something to entice Sarah with. "And my cross!" she announced triumphantly. "You can wear my cross. Anytime you want."

"You'd better not say that if you don't mean it," Caitlin warned. "What if she *is* hearing you?"

"I mean it."

Ever since Jenna had received her gold cross as a present, Sarah had been in love with it. She had begged to borrow it a hundred times, but Jenna had never let her. On the contrary, she had threatened her sister with dire consequences if she so much as touched it. If Sarah ever got her hands on the cross, she'd only be certain to lose it. Or so Jenna had thought. Now, faced with losing something more precious than gold, she regretted her selfishness. She could at least have let Sarah wear the cross to church. How was she going to lose it there, with the entire family watching? The truth was Jenna just hadn't wanted to share.

"I'm serious, Sarah," she said. "Give me a sign that you hear me, and you can wear it right now."

117

She and Caitlin both watched, straining to pick up the slightest movement. But Sarah remained completely unresponsive.

"She doesn't hear you," Caitlin said at last. "Or that would have had her for sure." Moving heavily, she sank back into her chair.

Jenna sat in the other one. "You don't know she doesn't hear," she said stubbornly, more for her own benefit than Caitlin's. "Maybe she just can't move."

"Maybe." Caitlin slipped her hand into the bag at her side and pulled out a book. "Want to try this?"

Jenna grabbed it. "Look, Sarah," she said, standing up to hold it over the unconscious girl. "Here's that book you were reading."

The book Sarah was holding when she was hit had been found in the bushes four yards over and brought to the hospital by a kind homeowner. Jenna didn't mention that part as she flipped through its pages, trying to guess where her sister had been.

"I don't know what page you were on, so I'll start near the beginning. Chapter two, all right? Stop me if you already read this part," she added, sitting back down to begin.

She heard her voice fill the room as she started, surprisingly calm and steady. But inside her heart was breaking.

Would Sarah even live long enough to reach the end of the story?

Nine

Peter felt shaky with uncertainty as he walked up behind Melanie after school on Friday, but he had to talk to someone who knew both him and Jenna. "Hi. Got a minute?"

Melanie turned around at her open locker, her face registering her surprise.

"I know. I should be at the hospital," he said quickly, anticipating her objection. "I'm going in a minute. Well, in a few minutes. Jenna's stopping by her house before she heads over there, so there's no big hurry. If you want, I can give you a lift home."

"Okay," she said slowly, obviously still confused. Closing her locker, she hoisted her backpack onto her shoulders.

"I just want to talk to you," he explained as they walked toward the exit door.

"About?"

"Nothing in particular, just . . ." He hesitated, terrified of seeming disloyal. But what good was a second opinion if he didn't come out with the facts? "It's Jenna," he admitted. "I'm really worried about her."

Melanie pushed the door open. "I can see why. She's in pretty bad shape."

"Exactly," he said, relieved.

He should have known Melanie would understand. When Eight Prime had first formed, back before he and Jenna had become a couple, he and Melanie had spent a lot of time together. He hadn't thought about it before, but with Jenna so wrapped up in family problems, he realized now that he missed those times. He couldn't really explain what the bond between him and Melanie had been, but there had definitely been a bond.

"I thought she'd snap out of it by now," Melanie continued. "I mean, I don't expect her to carry on like nothing is happening, but I thought she'd be a little more positive. I thought . . . well, to be honest I thought she'd be hoping and praying and telling *us* this would be okay, instead of the other way around."

"Exactly!" Peter repeated gratefully.

Hurrying ahead of her, he unlocked the door on the passenger side of his Toyota. Since his promise at Lent to save as much gas money as he could, he'd been doing his best, but with all the trips to the hospital a loop past Melanie's house wasn't going to make much difference. At least he was packing his lunch every day.

"I just wish I knew what she was feeling," he said, pulling out of the lot. "Has she said anything to you girls? I mean, anything she might not have said to me?"

Melanie shook her head. "Just that she's scared. But I'm sure you've heard that a hundred times."

"Well, not in so many words. She never actually said that to me."

"She figures you already know."

Maybe, he thought, driving in silence. But if Jenna was giving him credit for knowing what was going on in her head, then she was giving him way too much credit.

"I don't understand the way she's behaving," he admitted. "It's scary. And if Sarah dies . . ." He didn't even want to think about that. "I'm trying really hard, but I feel like I'm no help to her at all."

Melanie regarded him with amazement, a slight smile on her full lips. "You're kidding, right? You're like the perfect boyfriend, Peter."

"No, I'm not," he said irritably, not in the mood to be flattered. "She's shutting me out. She's shutting everyone out."

"Then you shouldn't take it personally."

"How can I *not* take it personally? I love her!"

Melanie turned her head abruptly, staring out the side window at the passing fields.

Oh, great. Now I've offended her. He hadn't meant his voice to be so sharp, but the whole situation was making him crazy. "I mean, don't you think it's personal?" he asked meekly.

121

"I don't know," she said at last, her eyes still on the landscape. "All I know is, you've been there for her every minute. If she doesn't appreciate that, she's crazy."

"Do you think . . . well, do you think she might be mad at me?"

"What? What for?"

"Just . . . can you think of any reason?"

"No. Of course not."

He sighed. "Me either."

The only possibility was that one kiss with Melanie he'd stupidly revealed on Valentine's Day. If he'd had any idea how Jenna was going to react, he never would have mentioned it. But she had said she forgave him, so it couldn't be that. Could it?

For a moment, he thought of telling Melanie about the fight their kiss had caused. But he and Melanie had never once discussed that moment since the autumn night it had happened. It would be too embarrassing to bring it up now. For both of them, probably.

Besides, he thought, *Jenna knows that kiss didn't mean anything. I told her a hundred times.*

He stole a sideways look at Melanie, who still seemed fascinated by the scenery, and felt an unexpected twinge. Not regret, exactly, but something nearly like it. She was just so beautiful, talented, intelligent . . . lost.

Maybe, if things had turned out differently with Jenna . . .

They didn't, he told himself quickly. *I love Jenna. That kiss meant nothing.*

He fixed his eyes straight ahead. *And even if it did, it's so over now.*

Miguel stopped at the reception desk in the hospital lobby. "Hi. Can you tell me where the personnel office is?"

"Downstairs in the basement. When you get off the elevator, make a left and walk to the end of the hall. You'll see the sign."

"Thanks."

Miguel's sweaty finger slipped on the button he pressed for the elevator, and he hoped he wouldn't have to shake someone's hand. His stomach was in knots as he rode down the single floor.

This is ridiculous, he thought, not sure his nervousness wasn't a sign that he ought to forget the whole thing. *All I'm going to do is ask if they have any openings. It's not like I'm interviewing for chief surgeon.*

He found the personnel office easily. Better still, he found two large bulletin boards in the hallway outside it. A variety of job listings was posted there for anyone to read. Slightly calmer at the realization that he might not have to talk to an actual person, he wiped his palms on his pants and settled in to study the prospects.

"Doctor, lab technician, nurse, nurse, nurse," he muttered to himself, scanning the openings. It wasn't until he was halfway through the first board that he understood what the PROFESSIONAL STAFF heading on top of it meant.

These are all the medical people. People with some sort of schooling, he realized. The other board was headed SERVICE AND SUPPORT. Miguel sidled over to it, hoping for better luck.

"Yep, here we go," he muttered.

The first several listings were for janitors. He persevered, scanning openings for food service workers, a variety of clerical staff, a gift shop cashier, and—exactly as he had predicted—a dishwasher. He ruled out the dishwasher and housekeeping positions immediately. The job he already had with Sabrina was so much better that he couldn't even consider those. He didn't want to work with food, either. How would he learn anything useful about the hospital stuck in the kitchen? The cashier was probably the best choice. At least the gift shop was off the main lobby, right in the middle of things.

He read that opening carefully. "Minimum wage," he groaned. "*And* full time."

The cashier was out. That left clerical. He didn't know how to type, but maybe he could file or answer the phones or something. Not that being a secretary was what he'd had in mind.

What did *you have in mind, then? You knew it would have to be something like that.*

There seemed to be a couple of fairly unskilled

openings on the clerical staff. The pay was presented as a range, but he couldn't tell what the hours were. The way the ads were worded, he got the impression they might be pretty flexible. Steeling himself, he opened the office door and approached the first desk he saw.

"I was wondering," he announced, too loudly. The woman at the desk looked up at him, and so did men at the next two. "Um, I was wondering about the ads for clerical help you have posted outside," he said in a lower voice. "Was there someone I could talk to about that, or . . . ?"

"You need to fill out an application." Walking her fingers through a file drawer, the receptionist located something near the back and handed it to him. "Make sure you fill it out *completely* and provide the additional items—copies of your driver's license and social security card. When it's ready, you can either turn it in here, or mail it to the address on top. All right?"

"Yes, but . . . Isn't there someone I can talk to to find out more about the jobs?"

She shook her head. "That's not how it works. The jobs on the boards are a sampling of what we have, but things change all the time. What will happen is that your application will come in, it will go to the clerical supervisor, and if she has anything that fits your qualifications, she'll give you a call. You can discuss the position then."

"And the pay?"

"That'll depend on the job they have and your experience."

"So . . . I'm applying for a job, and I don't even know what it is?"

She laughed. "I suppose you could say that, but you're really just applying to be in our pool of candidates. Does that make sense?"

"I guess so. Sure."

It didn't, but he didn't want anyone to think he was a troublemaker. He left the office with the application clutched in his hand, completely confused. At least when he applied for a construction job, he knew what he'd be doing if he got it. And what he'd be getting paid.

Anything I'd get at the hospital is bound to pay a whole lot less than I make with Sabrina, no matter what, he thought, discouraged.

He walked out across the parking lot to his car, trying to remember what Leah had said about having to start over sometime if he was going to switch careers. But it was easy to make hypothetical statements over burgers and fries—being faced with the reality of an actual pay cut was something else entirely.

And it's not like clerical help is the job of my dreams. I don't even know anything about it.

He opened his rusty car door and threw the application on the cracked passenger seat. Dusk was falling, and the temperature had already plunged.

Miguel's cold fingers fumbled the key into the ignition as he hurried to start the engine. Instead of the expected roar, however, the engine cranked a few sickly times, then died.

"Perfect!" he exclaimed sarcastically.

It sounded like the battery was going out. He sat still a moment, trying to remember how old it was. *Old, that's for sure.*

He tried and failed to start the car again, then again, becoming increasingly upset as the engine cranked more and more slowly. If he couldn't get it going, he'd have to find someone to give him a jump, and he didn't have any cables. Worse, it was Friday evening, almost dinnertime, and the whole parking lot had cleared except for a few scattered cars. He could be out there waiting for help a long time.

On his fourth try, Miguel set the car rolling down the inclined parking lot, then popped it into gear. The engine coughed reluctantly to life and he stomped on the gas, his heart pounding with relief. He'd have to drive straight to the gas station to find out what was wrong, but that sure beat the alternative.

At least tomorrow is Saturday, he thought as he headed toward a station with an on-site mechanic. *I can work on the car in the morning, if I have to.* Sabrina had him on a shift in the afternoon, though, so if he couldn't get the engine running he'd have to find another way downtown.

What a pain. I hope it's only the battery. If it is, I'll buy a new one at the station.

That should take care of the problem—not that he was looking forward to the expense. A battery would set him back at least fifty dollars.

And that's assuming it is the battery. There were plenty of other parts to break in a car's electrical system. What if he had to buy a new starter, or he had a short or something?

"Isn't timing everything?" he asked, acutely aware of the blank application on the seat beside him. A few minutes before, filling it out had seemed like a bad idea. Now it seemed impossible.

What had he been thinking, anyway? Maybe having dreams was all right for other people. Other people could afford them.

Nicole scanned the menu nervously, wondering what she could order that didn't have a million calories. Everything looked delicious, but all the plates being carried past their table were full to overflowing. If she left half her food untouched, would Guy be upset with her?

"I know things aren't too fancy here, but the food's real good and I figured I couldn't go wrong with American," Guy said, picking up on her hesitation. "I hope they have something you like."

"I'm sure they do. In fact, I see lots of things," she said, searching in vain for a main-course salad. Was it totally forbidden to ask a guy to split a meal? She had a feeling it was.

"I know you were probably expecting me to take you somewhere more deluxe, like Wienerageous," Guy teased. "But being as—"

"I'll have the fried chicken," Nicole announced quickly, not wanting to hear another word about Wienerageous. *If I'm going off the calorie deep end, I might as well take the high dive.*

"The chicken is good. Plus you get three side dishes: mashed potatoes with gravy, baked beans, and macaroni and cheese. Oh, and a salad."

"Super," said Nicole, mustering up what she hoped was an enthusiastic smile.

The waitress came and took their order, leaving behind a basket that Guy immediately picked up. "Bread?" he offered, trying to pass it to her.

"I'd better save room. They serve so much more food than I usually eat that I don't even think I'll be able to finish my dinner."

"I won't be surprised if you don't," he said. "It *is* a lot of food."

She smiled slightly, relieved—until she remembered she was supposed to work Courtney and Jeff into the conversation. Her gut started twisting again. Why had she ever agreed to Courtney's stupid plan in the first place? The whole situation was awkward enough without that added pressure.

But she had to do her best or Courtney would be

mad. She stirred the ice around in her soda, trying to think of an opening.

"So. This is kind of unexpected, isn't it? I never would have guessed after that first blind date with Courtney and Jeff that we'd end up together here."

Guy looked at her strangely, then went ahead and laughed. "To say the least."

"How *is* Jeff these days?

"He goes to your school. You probably see him more often than I do."

"Um, sure. From a distance. But ever since he and Courtney—"

"Oh. I see where this is going."

The knowing look on his face nearly gave her a heart attack. "You do?"

"Sure. You see him, but you don't talk to him anymore." Guy helped himself to a second roll. "If you're sure you don't want any . . . ," he said, holding it up.

"No. Go ahead."

The waitress reappeared and put down two salads. Nicole ate a few bites of hers without dressing, wondering if she ought to try again or drop the subject of Jeff while she could. Guy was sure to catch on if she made the slightest mistake, and then what would he think? That she only went out with him again as another favor to Courtney?

I wish I'd never even told Courtney we had a date, Nicole thought miserably, feeling completely stressed out. After everything she and Guy had gone through to get to this point, she didn't need any more misunderstandings.

"Courtney talked to Jeff the other day," Nicole said nervously. "Just the one time, but I guess they're making up. I mean, there are no hard feelings, right?"

Guy nodded. "Why should there be?"

"Right. There shouldn't." At least she'd made that much progress. But it wasn't enough. Courtney was sure to be upset if she didn't try a little harder. Taking a deep breath, Nicole braced for another question. "Do, uh . . . do you and Jeff double-date a lot?"

"No," he said, snickering. "Why?"

"I just wondered, you know, if you guys went out a lot. Or if it was just the one time. Not that it *matters*. I was just, you know, curious."

I sound like a total moron! she wailed silently. *If Courtney were here, she'd kill me.*

Guy studied her over his salad. "I don't go out a lot, Nicole . . . and I'm not seeing anyone else right now. Is that what you want to know?"

He thinks I'm checking up on him! she realized, horrified. She would never be so lame as to be jealous on a first date—even a second first date. *Courtney, you're on your own!* If there was to be any more discussion of Jeff that night, Guy would have to start it.

"Um, no. Not really. But it's, uh, nice to hear," she said, grateful to spot her chicken arriving. She dug into the down-home meal, the food providing the ultimate change of subject. "Ooh, these beans are delicious!"

Guy had ordered the open-face steak sandwich: two huge slabs of crusty bread under a juicy steak. Coleslaw, fries, and fruit salad competed for space on the rest of the platter. "I told you they had good food," he said happily.

The talk through dinner was mostly of the getting-to-know-you variety. They talked about their schools, their siblings, their favorite places to hang out during the summer. It seemed odd to start with such basics when they'd met so long before, but they still didn't know each other too well. Nicole gradually found herself studying Guy as he spoke, strangely taken in by his unruly auburn hair, expressively earnest blue eyes, and quick smile. She thought she could almost feel the beginning of something . . . something . . .

"I have my guitar out in the trunk," he announced when the waitress brought the check. "I thought after this maybe we could swing past the hospital and see Sarah. I'll play her that song Jenna likes."

Whatever Nicole thought she'd been feeling disappeared faster than cash at the mall. Singing to the sick? How corny! Not to mention that on a Saturday night the entire Conrad family would probably be there to witness her embarrassment.

"I'm, uh, not sure they'll let you play guitar in the hospital."

He smiled. "Don't worry. It's not my electric guitar."

That was the least of her worries, actually. She kept hoping he wasn't serious as they left the restaurant and drove to the hospital. With each mile that ticked past her window, though, the person behind the wheel seemed more like the loser she'd first met than the cute guy she'd just had dinner with. All Nicole could think about was how painfully goody-goody Guy was sometimes—and what Courtney would say if she ever found out they'd spent their big date singing.

I will take that information to my grave, she promised herself.

She tagged along a couple of steps behind him as he strode through the hospital lobby, his guitar slung over his back.

"What floor is it again?" he asked inside the elevator, his finger hovering over the buttons.

She leaned forward and pushed it herself.

"You've gotten awfully quiet," he said as they rode up. "Worried about Sarah?"

She managed a weak smile. *Yeah. That's it.*

There was no one at the nurses' station, so the guitar went by without remark, dashing Nicole's last hope. They walked down the hall to Sarah's room, where the door stood partially open.

"Nicole!" Mrs. Conrad greeted her. "How nice of you to come."

Despite Nicole's prediction, only half of the Conrads were there. Mrs. Conrad and Jenna had the chairs by the bed, while Caitlin had managed to locate a third one somewhere and tuck it away in the corner. She waved as Nicole and Guy walked in.

"Hi," said Nicole. "I don't think you met Guy when we were here last weekend."

"Nice to meet you, Guy. Jenna's told us all about you hearing you play in Los Angeles. Look, Jenna, Guy brought his guitar."

Jenna rose slowly from her chair. "Are you going to play? Do you think you could play a song for Sarah?"

"That's why we're here," he said, flashing Nicole a conspirator's smile.

"Here, take my chair," Jenna said, pulling it even closer to the bed. "You can sit right here."

Guy sat down and began tuning his guitar, while Caitlin rose to close the door.

"I can't believe he came to sing for us," Jenna backed up to tell Nicole, grateful tears filling her blue eyes. "I hope . . . oh, I really hope Sarah can hear."

Then Guy began to play softly, and when he began to sing, everything stopped but the sound of his voice. Nicole found herself back at the concert in L.A., reliving her first stunned realization that this boy she had scorned was a gifted musician. She remembered the frenzied screams that had accompanied his onstage appearance, and the looks of envy from the other girls when they found out Nicole knew him. She had understood then that she'd been a fool to judge him so quickly. Now, seeing a flicker of reassurance on Jenna's face, she realized she'd done it again. Guy's song, the embarrassing gesture she'd been so annoyed by, meant a lot to her hurting friend.

I'm such a baby, she told herself. *I don't even deserve him.*

Which was assuming too much, she suddenly realized. How did she know this wasn't a one-time thing? What made her think he'd ask to see her again?

He has to, she decided. She didn't know what kind of relationship she and Guy had, or if it was headed anywhere, but watching him now, his head bent over his guitar, she knew she wasn't ready for it to be over.

If he doesn't ask me, then I'll ask him.

Ten

Melanie pushed Sarah's door open cautiously, feeling like an intruder. She had expected that at least some of the Conrads would be at the hospital that Sunday morning, but the desk nurse had just told her they'd all gone to church. Sarah's room was silent except for the ventilator, and Melanie crept slowly toward the bed, afraid to make any noise.

"Hi, Sarah. Remember me?" she whispered, bending over the still girl. "How are you feeling today?"

Sarah gave no sign she'd heard, but her appearance answered for her. Wan and thin, she seemed to slip farther away every day.

"Not too good, huh?" Lifting the edge of the blanket, Melanie found a hand to hold.

"I hope at least you're not hurting. When I was unconscious in the hospital, I had all these strange dreams, but no pain at all. I was actually kind of sorry to wake up."

She gazed down at the sleeping girl, wondering if Sarah was lost somewhere in the same warm place. "Of course, I wasn't as hurt as you are."

Melanie glanced toward the door, to make sure they were unobserved, then lowered her voice even further. "I'll tell you a secret, but you have to promise not to tell anyone else. When I was unconscious like you are, I had the weirdest feeling that someone was watching over me the whole time. I thought it was Peter Altmann, but later I found out that he'd only been around off and on. And then, when I woke up, I saw this woman bending over my bed, just the way I'm doing now, and she reached out her hand like this . . ."

Gently, carefully, Melanie brought the backs of her fingers to Sarah's forehead, stroking gently from temple to temple. Sarah's skin felt hot and dry, as if she had a fever.

"I thought she was my mom," Melanie admitted. "Except that my mom is dead. Peter thinks I saw an angel, but I don't know. What do you think, Sarah? Did you ever see an angel?"

She waited a moment, not really expecting an answer.

"Probably not," she said with a sigh. "I'll bet you believe in them, though, don't you? Your whole family believes in them, I'll bet."

Letting go of Sarah's hand, Melanie leaned against the cold steel rail of the bed, lost in thought. "I don't know what I believe. I thought by now I'd have forgotten all about that lady, or at least figured out what she was. I mean, was she a dream? Was I

137

hallucinating? I did crack my head pretty hard. But it all just seemed so real." She held a forearm out over the bed. "Look. Goose bumps. That was probably the strangest thing that's ever happened to me. I'll tell you something, though . . ."

She glanced toward the door again, then crouched to whisper between the rails. "I'd give anything to know it was real. To know *she* was real."

Melanie dropped into a chair at Sarah's bedside, suddenly drained. Melanie had woken up that morning full of energy, and almost immediately she had decided to bike to the hospital. At the time it had just seemed like a friendly thing to do, but now she wondered if something more had drawn her there. Was she trying to relive her own near-death experience through Sarah's? Yearning for that moment when she thought she had seen her mother?

Her mother. Melanie leaned back in the chair and closed her eyes. In a way, reading her mother's diary was opening more questions than it closed. She had read the entries up through midsummer now, and, knowing how her mother's life had eventually turned out, she couldn't see any way to get from the facts to the completely separate reality being described by a teenage Tristyn.

By mid-July, Tristyn and Trent were still madly in love, even more so than before. Their relationship had become so intense, in fact, that Tristyn's fights with her parents were worse. In an effort to distract her from what they considered a dangerous romance, they had tried to force her to join a youth group at their church. Tristyn had gone only once, then announced that she would not attend again—and she wasn't going to Sunday services anymore either.

"I have better things to do than waste half the day jawing with a bunch of old hypocrites," she'd shouted at the height of the ensuing fight with her mother. "To hear you people tell it, you've all been perfect your whole lives, and I'm the worst thing that ever lived. Well, I'm not bad, I'm a teenager! I'm *normal*! And I'll see Trent as much as I want to."

The next day, Tristyn had moved the diary to Lisa's house, too paranoid to keep it in her room at home. She was convinced that her parents would read it if they found it, and as the hours she spent with Trent grew more numerous they had too many opportunities. It was much harder to make entries when she had to retrieve the book from her friend's house first, but having it out of her parents' reach was the only way Tristyn could sleep. Melanie remembered part of what her mother had written:

I should probably just get rid of this book altogether. Burn it or something—that would be safest. But now that I've put so much time into writing it, I hate to throw it away. It's like it belongs to me and

*Trent now, and years from now, when I'm older,
I know I'll want to look back on this summer as
the happiest time of my life. Except for the has-
sles with Mom and Dad. I don't know why they
can't just accept that I'm not a little girl anymore!
If they wouldn't push so hard, I wouldn't push
them away.*

With a sigh, Melanie rose from the chair. Whatever had happened to Trent? And were these the
fights that Tristyn and her parents had never made
up? This petty high-school stuff? She'd have to finish reading to find out.

"Well, Sarah, I guess I'm going to go," she said
softly. "I'm on my bike, and it looks like it might start
raining. You hang in there, okay? Everyone's pulling
for you."

Everyone's praying for you, she almost added, but
with a slight shake of her head she turned and
walked out the door.

That wasn't for her to say.

"Jenna!" said Reverend Thompson. "Come in."

She hesitated in his office doorway, full of misgivings. She had talked to her pastor hundreds of times,
more than she could count. Between all the services
and other church activities she'd attended, she felt
like she knew him well. But she had never sought

him out privately before. That was something adults usually did. Adults with serious problems.

"Come in," he repeated, standing to motion her to a chair. "Please. Are you by yourself?"

"Yes," she said, moving slowly to the large leather armchair across from his cluttered desk. The desk was piled with books, while shelves on all four walls bowed under similar loads. A single large window let light into the room, making the space seem more cozy than crowded. "Everyone else went home to get lunch before they go to the hospital," she explained. "But I wanted . . . I mean I was wondering . . ."

She didn't even know how to say it. How could she tell the man who had baptized her that his sermon that day had left her cold? Again. That she was questioning everything she'd ever believed in? That if Sarah died she didn't know how she could live? She knew she was in trouble. She knew she needed help. She just didn't know how to ask for it.

"I was wondering . . ." She tried again. "I mean, why do you think this happened? Why Sarah? She's just a little kid." Jenna's voice shook and she was afraid she was going to cry, but she had to ask the question. If a pastor couldn't explain this, who could?

Reverend Thompson nodded as if he had expected something similar, and left the chair behind his desk to take the one at her side. He'd grown old in his vocation, and his hair was completely silver. His eyes met hers, kind and wise, and for a moment she felt a glimmer of hope.

"You don't know how God could do this to your little sister, and you want me to give you the reason," he said, pushing her hopes still higher.

Then he sighed. "I wish I could."

She stared at him in disbelief. That was all? That was the best he had to offer?

He seemed to read her thoughts. "It's situations like this that test our faith. If God is good, and he knows everything about everyone, then it only makes sense that good things should happen to good people and bad things should happen to bad ones. It makes sense, but it isn't always the case. And when things go the other way, we feel betrayed. Theologians have been trying to explain this forever, and better men than I have failed. Which is to say that explanations are reached—but we still feel betrayed. Is that how you feel?"

"Yes," she said wonderingly, amazed that he could put a word on the confusion inside her so quickly. "It feels like God's turned against me, or at least forgotten who I am. And I want to feel like I did before, the way I used to when he still cared, but I can't."

Tears poured down her face, but the words were finally flowing and she had to let them out. "It's like I don't even know him anymore. And no matter how hard I try, I can't . . ." She gulped for air through her sobs. "I can't find him. He's not there."

"But he is." Reaching across the space between their chairs, the minister took her hands in his. "He *is* there, Jenna. And now is when you need him most. Have faith and let him comfort you."

"I can't," she whimpered. "It's too hard."

"It can be hard sometimes. Sometimes we have to fight for our faith. But faith doesn't mean believing everything will turn out the way we want it to, or even the way we think it should. Sometimes it's enough just to believe that God is good."

"I—I do believe that," she stammered. "But I still don't know why this happened. All I can think is that it's my fault, that I caused it somehow. If I had only—"

"No," he interrupted gently. "I don't know why Sarah is suffering, but it's surely a mistake to take this onto yourself. Sarah's accident is not your fault. I'm one hundred percent certain of that."

"But maybe to get my attention, or teach me a lesson . . . ," she faltered.

"Sarah is as important to God as you are. Do you really think he would use her that way just to teach you a lesson?"

It made no sense at all when he put it like that. "No?" she replied hopefully.

"Of course not." He shook his silver head. "I don't

have all the answers, Jenna, but I do know this. God loves you. And he loves your sister. Put your trust in him with the certainty that, whatever happens, God is in charge, and God knows what he's doing." He smiled a little ruefully. "Even when we don't."

"You're right," she heard herself saying. And suddenly everything rushed up inside her, as if a weight had been lifted. "No, I mean you're *really* right. Oh, thank you, Reverend Thompson. Thank you so much!"

She pushed her hair off her wet face and rose to her feet. "I have to go, but thanks. You really helped." Hesitating only a second, she turned and ran for the door.

The sky outside was cold and gray as Jenna started the long walk home, but to her the world seemed beautiful. Her nose filled with the scents of pine and rain, as intense as if newly invented. Every cloud was edged with light, every field with rich brown soil. It felt as if her senses had been living underwater, cut off from the world. Now they broke up through the surface, astonishing her with their sharpness. She grabbed at some weeds on the side of the road just to feel them slide through her fingers. She tilted her head to listen: a chorus of birds, a barking dog, and, somewhere far away, the sound of a little child laughing. And before she could stop she was laughing too, bubbling over with the hope welling up inside her.

"I can't believe it!" she cried, opening her arms to the sky. "I never knew hope happens like this, just because you need it to."

And the tears that wet her cheeks this time were full of awe and joy. Suddenly God didn't seem so far away at all.

"So what are we going to see?" Leah asked excitedly, climbing into the car beside Miguel. "I can't believe we're actually going to do something together in broad daylight."

"You're exaggerating," he said, making a face as he pulled away from the curb. "It's not that bad."

It is too, she retorted silently. He worked nearly every afternoon now, and most weekends. On Saturday he hadn't started work until one, but he'd spent all morning going over his car engine, making sure everything was working and trying to head off more expenses, like the battery he'd had to replace on Friday.

"Checking stuff doesn't keep it from breaking," she'd complained, wanting to spend time with him. "Batteries wear out no matter what you do."

But there was no arguing when he had set his mind on something, so his ungrateful car had gotten the attention instead of her.

"How about that new comedy?" she proposed now. "What's it called?"

"It had better be called *A Dollar Per Ticket*,"

Miguel grumbled, peering at the gauges on his dashboard as if he expected them all to go haywire any second. "This has already been an expensive weekend."

"I'll pay," Leah said quickly. "It was my idea, so it's my treat."

Miguel looked far from grateful. "I hate it when you pay."

"Tough." Leaning forward, she flipped on the car radio and spun through the dial, trying to find a station. "So, did you take your application back to the hospital yet?"

"No, I didn't take it back. I don't even know if I'll fill it out. I can't afford to change jobs."

"You don't know until you try."

"I do too, Leah. Were you paying attention at all last night when I explained this over the phone?"

"Yes," she said impatiently. He didn't have any money. His family didn't have any money. None of the clerical jobs paid any money. She was *sick* of hearing about money, especially since his mother seemed far less concerned about it than he did. "Did you ask your mother what she thinks you should do?"

"I don't need to ask my mother. It's my decision."

"I think if you just ask her—"

"If I ask her, she'll tell me to do whatever I want. And since that's exactly what I'm going to do anyway, what's the point? Are we going to talk about this all day?"

"Not unless you want to."

"I don't."

"Fine."

She crossed her arms and settled back into her seat, silent as Miguel drove to the theater. As rude as he'd just been, she figured she had to at least pretend to sulk a few minutes. But she wasn't really angry. She wasn't even that discouraged. Hadn't he just said he'd do whatever he wanted? And he wanted to work at the hospital. It was simply a matter of time before he admitted it.

Is there a hospital near Stanford? she wondered, pretending to glare out the window. If he was switching jobs anyway, there couldn't be any good reason left to stay in Clearwater Crossing. The hospitals in California were probably bigger, and if Miguel left home his mother and Rosa could be perfectly comfortable in a two-bedroom apartment, which would cost a lot less than the three-bedroom he'd been saving for.

Of course, he was still going to need to start college as soon as possible. But why couldn't he go to school in California too? If he couldn't get into Stanford, there had to be plenty of other good schools. Of course, if he *could* get into Stanford . . .

I wonder if they have a medical school? she thought dreamily.

She didn't know, but she definitely intended to find out.

Eleven

"All right, already! I already knew there were no hard feelings. Did Guy say Jeff's going to call me or what?" Courtney picked restlessly at the soft bread of her otherwise untouched sandwich. "Come *on*, Nicole."

"I think you're dragging this out on purpose," Emily accused from across the cafeteria table.

Nicole lowered her diet soda. "Why would I do that?" she asked innocently, feeling like she finally had the edge in their weird triangle. All through lunch that Monday she'd been parceling out what little she'd learned about Jeff in tiny bits and pieces, doing her best to drive Emily crazy by monopolizing Courtney's attention.

It was working, too.

"I'm waiting," Courtney said impatiently, with an irritated glance at Emily for interrupting.

"I thought you didn't *want* me to ask Guy to tell Jeff to call you."

There was a hint of exasperation in Courtney's

eyes. "Not in so many words! You were supposed to hint around."

"Exactly. You wanted me to be subtle, and I was." Nicole lifted her soda again and took a long, slow drink. She took her time putting the can back down, then leaned toward Courtney, lowering her voice. "I know he's not dating anyone else, though."

"I knew it!" Courtney crowed.

"That's great, Courtney!" Emily added excitedly. But her presence was extraneous and all three of them knew it.

"So then why hasn't he called me?" Courtney wondered aloud. "Why is he acting so shy?"

"He's probably embarrassed," Nicole guessed. "He knows he blew it, and now he's not sure if you'll take him back. I'd go slow too, if I were him."

"You're right!" Courtney said. "How perfect."

Nicole smiled. "All I know is, he and Guy haven't been on a single double date since that time they went out with us."

"But . . . that doesn't mean anything," Emily protested, quick to spot the flaw. "Just because Jeff isn't going out with Guy doesn't mean he isn't going out with girls."

"I think we can *assume* that if Jeff were seeing someone, Guy would have mentioned it," said Nicole, all ready with her reply. "It only makes sense."

"Yeah, Emily," said Courtney, annoyed. "Why do you have to shoot everything down?"

"I—I'm not shooting down," Emily sputtered in self-defense. "But what if Guy didn't *know* Jeff was—"

"I can see how you would say that, since you've never met either of them." Nicole made sure her voice was even more condescending than Emily's always was to her. "But Courtney and I know them really well, so I *think* we're in a better position to judge."

"Yeah, Emily," Courtney repeated. "If you don't know what you're talking about, the least you can do is shut up."

Emily glared at Nicole, then down at the greasy gravy on her tray. Nicole could feel her stewing as she plotted her revenge.

Plot away! Nicole thought happily. *I've got you now and you know it.*

Because as long as Courtney was obsessed with Jeff—and Nicole was the only one with information about him—Nicole had the upper hand. No amount of bribes or concert tickets could change that.

"Why don't you come over again some night this week?" Nicole invited Courtney. "I'll ask my mom to make that chocolate pudding cake you like."

"Wow, I can't even remember the last time I had that. It's been too long."

"Way too long," Nicole agreed, smirking at Emily.

* * *

"I, uh, I have this application to turn in," Miguel said hesitantly, handing it over the desk to the personnel office receptionist. "I think everything's there," he added as she flipped through his paper-clipped pages.

"Looks like it." The woman tossed his packet into a plastic tray marked IN. "Let's see . . . this is Tuesday? It usually takes a week or two for applications to be processed. Then, if we have anything to offer you, you'll get a call. So don't expect to hear before next Wednesday, at the earliest."

"Should I . . . should I check back or something?" Miguel asked. "I could call here in a couple of days."

"You could, but we won't know anything more. You need to wait to hear. If they decide to interview you, you'll be the first to find out."

"Okay, then. Thanks." Miguel backed through the office doorway and closed the door behind him, full of misgivings. It had been hard enough to make up his mind to apply for a job at the hospital. If they made him wait very long . . .

This whole thing is crazy, he thought, walking down the hall toward the elevator. *Even if they offer me a job, I still don't know if I'll take it.*

How could he? With a cut in pay that big, he'd have to work even more hours than he was already pulling with Sabrina, which meant that playing water polo this season was definitely out of the question. Not only that, but he hated the thought of delaying his family's move out of public housing, even by one day. Discouraged, he punched the Up elevator button, waiting distractedly until the double doors opened.

I'll just stop in to see Sarah for a minute, he told himself as the elevator car began its ascent. *Since I'm already here. Again.*

When Miguel stepped out on Sarah's floor, the quiet in the waiting room was so pronounced he was almost afraid to speak to the nurse behind the desk. She took his name, then pointed him down a hall to Sarah's room. Just as he was about to enter, however, the door opened from inside and a doctor walked into the hall.

"How is she today?" asked Miguel, keeping his voice low. "Is there any improvement yet?"

The man, whose white coat identified him as Dr. Malone, seemed surprised to be stopped. His dark brows bunched together as he tried to place Miguel.

"I'm a friend of the family," Miguel explained quickly. "Of her sister, Jenna. I was just hoping . . . maybe . . ."

The doctor shook his head. "No change. I'm sorry."

And Miguel could see he was. Compassion showed in the man's brown eyes, the jut of his jaw, and even the way his shoulders slumped.

Dr. Malone drew a deep breath. "We're not giving up, though. Not for a second. She's young, and she's small, but she's stronger than she looks or she

152

wouldn't have made it this far. Things could still change for the better."

Could they still change for the worse? Miguel wondered, but he kept his question to himself. "Have you seen a lot of patients like Sarah?" he asked instead. "I mean, people in comas?"

The doctor nodded, a faraway expression creeping onto his face. "Coma is one of the most frustrating things I deal with, and at the same time one of the most fascinating. The brain is just so complex, and we know so little about it. Sarah could wake up five minutes from now and be completely fine. Or there could be damage I have no way of predicting. Conversely, she could wake up a long, long way down the road. Or never. That's the nature of coma. It's unpredictable."

Even though the subject was grim, Dr. Malone spoke with passion, his love for his work shining through every word. And in that moment none of Miguel's fears seemed to matter anymore. Being a doctor was an important job—one he wanted to do. How could playing water polo or even having a private apartment ever compare to saving lives?

"I want to be a doctor too," Miguel found himself blurting out. "My father . . . died of cancer. For a while, I was really bitter. But then my mom, she needed a kidney transplant and she got one at this hospital. It totally changed our lives. And ever since then, I knew. I mean, I wanted . . . well, there just isn't another job like it, is there?"

Dr. Malone smiled. "No. There really isn't."

Miguel nodded eagerly. "That's what I thought. I don't know what it's going to take for me to become a doctor, and I don't know if I can afford it, but I want to try. In fact, I just turned in an application downstairs to see if I can get a job here."

"What kind of job?" the doctor asked curiously.

"Clerical help," Miguel admitted, looking down at his worn boots. "I actually have a better job already, but I thought if I was working here in the hospital, I could learn a lot more about everything, and find out if this is really what I want to pursue."

"Are you still in high school?"

"Yes, and that's another problem. I can't work full time."

"Then why not apply for our teen internship program? It probably pays about the same as entry-level clerical work, and you'll learn a lot more than you would pushing papers around in the basement."

"Your teen what?" said Miguel, snapping his gaze back up. "No one downstairs told me anything about that."

"It's not something we advertise, because it's not a regular job and we have such limited funds. Just once in a while, when the right person comes along . . . The whole thing is designed for kids like you, actually—high school students who want to learn about careers in medicine. If you get in, your supervisor will work around your school schedule, which is more than the clerical department will do. You ought to check it out. Drop back by Personnel and ask for the application."

"I will," Miguel promised. In fact, it was all he could do to keep from turning and sprinting straight to the elevator. "I definitely will."

"You'll need to write an essay, and I think you have to get a letter of recommendation from a practicing physician. Maybe the one who oversaw your mother's transplant?"

"Dr. Gibbons?" Miguel's mind was racing with newfound hope. The two of them hadn't always seen eye to eye, but in the end they had made up their differences. There was no way she could say Miguel had been anything but supportive and responsible all through his mother's long illness. "I'm certain she'll recommend me."

"Well, I wish you the best of luck," Dr. Malone said with a smile. "Perhaps I'll see you around again sometime."

"Oh, you'll see me," Miguel said determinedly as he reached to open Sarah's door. He knew now he'd just stay a minute before heading back downstairs.

You'll see me one way or another.

Jenna checked her watch, then pulled her chair closer to Sarah's bedside, resting her head against her sister's arm.

"It's getting pretty late," she murmured. "Caitlin'll

be here soon, and then I'll have to go home. I have to get some sleep before that stupid geography test tomorrow."

She yawned without bothering to cover her mouth, seeing the books and papers on the floor through bleary eyes. "It sure is quiet in here without the ventilator."

Dr. Malone had taken Sarah off the machine that afternoon, after performing periodic tests to make sure she was breathing properly. At first Jenna had been elated. Then she had learned it didn't mean much. The coma wasn't preventing Sarah from breathing—coma patients sometimes breathed on their own for years. The ventilation had been primarily for Sarah's flail chest: ribs so severely broken that segments had been isolated from the rib cage. Now, twelve days after the accident, Sarah's ribs had healed sufficiently for her to breathe on her own, with only a thin, clear tube carrying additional oxygen to her nose. There was still no telling when— or if—her brain might catch up with her bones, though.

I never thought I'd miss that awful sound, Jenna thought, strangely unnerved by the quiet. In a sad, desperate way, the wheeze of forced breathing had become reassuring. Instead of despairing, however, Jenna snuggled closer to her sister.

Whatever happens, the future is up to God, she thought, more certain of that than she'd ever been.

Scooting around in her chair a little, she took Sarah's hand through the blanket.

"You want to pray, Sarah?" she asked. "Caitlin's going to sleep here tonight instead of Dad, so let's you and I say our prayers together. 'Our Father, who art in heaven . . .' "

She spoke slowly, deliberately, as if to let Sarah jump in and join her. Sarah didn't respond, but as Jenna continued with the Lord's Prayer she had the sudden sense that she wasn't praying alone, that she was being swept up into a safe, warm current much larger and stronger than she was.

How could *I* be praying alone? she realized. All over the world, thousands of people were sure to be saying the same prayer, so many that she was almost certain to be praying in exact sync with someone else. Maybe with a hundred someones. It was like being in church, in a way. Closing her eyes, Jenna relaxed into the feeling, relying on that unseen community.

She wasn't alone. More importantly, Sarah wasn't alone. Whatever happened here on Earth, somehow they would bear it. And they *would* be together again, in a place where they could never be parted.

Jenna lifted her head, her voice rising with conviction. " 'For thine is the kingdom, and the power, and the glory, forever. Amen.' "

157

Twelve

"No way!" Melanie gasped "No way!"

She glanced from her mother's diary toward her open bedroom door, then quickly got up to shut it. School had barely let out that Wednesday, and it was still early enough for her father to stumble upstairs. Falling back onto her bed, she eagerly began reading the shocking entry:

> Trent asked me to marry him! I'm so excited! I had almost given up hope, with college supposed to start in a week. Mom and Dad are actually marking off the days on a calendar by the kitchen phone—like I didn't already know they can't wait to see me and Trent separated. Before this summer I never would have believed they could stoop to something so juvenile.
>
> But anyway! He asked me last night. We were up at the pond, just hanging out, and he said, "When I go to Clearwater University next week, why don't you come with me?" At first I didn't know what he meant. I told him I couldn't, I'd al-

ready been accepted to Syracuse. "You could transfer," he said, dropping little kisses all over my face.
Believe me, right then I _wanted_ to transfer, but you
can't transfer when you haven't even started yet,
and it's way too late to apply as a new freshman
now. Besides, my parents would never pay for _that_
change of plans—not in a million years.

"So then just come and forget about school," he
said. "What do you need college for? We're going
to get married, aren't we?" "Are we?" I said, and I
could barely hear my own voice, my heart was
pounding so hard. "We never talked about it." You
should have seen the wounded look he gave me—it
was so adorable. "Does that mean no?" A second
later I was kissing him for all I was worth. Who
cares about college anyway? Not me. Not when I
can be with Trent.

So now we've got it all figured out. Well, almost
all figured out. I'll take a job in Clearwater Crossing while Trent goes to college, and once he gets his
teaching credential he'll be a coach and support us
while we raise a family. A mom is the only thing I
ever really wanted to be anyway. I hope we have a
little girl first. Trent wants boys, of course, but I
can't imagine anything more perfect than a daughter all my own. The only thing left is to find out
how to elope in a hurry. It will have to be an elopement, because there isn't nearly enough time to
plan a wedding before we leave, and I can't move in

with Trent if we aren't married. I mean, I could, but I might want my parents to speak to me again sometime before I die. We'll have to go out of town, because two minutes after we started asking questions about marriage licenses here our entire families would know. It's not going to be what I pictured—the white dress, the walk down the aisle—but so what? Getting married is only for a few minutes anyway; being married is for a life-time. That's what counts, not the ceremony. Trent's supposed to find out how to do it without anyone catching on. Just think! In a few days, I'll be Mrs. Trent Wheeler. I can't believe it!

"I can't believe it either," Melanie said, rolling over onto her back.

Never, in all her life before the diary, had Melanie so much as heard the name Trent Wheeler. Now she was supposed to believe this guy was the reason her mother had left Iowa to move to Clearwater Crossing? The mere possibility was mind-boggling. And if she had married Trent, what had happened to him? Did they get divorced?

"Impossible!" Melanie sat up abruptly. "It's impossible that my mom was divorced and I never knew about it. More likely they never even got married."

That had to be it. Everything was against them. Eloping wasn't even a good plan. Giving up college to follow some guy? If her mother hadn't been so blinded by love, she never would have considered it. Besides, Melanie knew that her mother *had* gone to college and earned a degree in art. She'd gone to CU, in fact.

"They probably changed their minds," she guessed, although that still didn't explain how Tristyn had ended up in Missouri. Melanie had barely flipped the page, though, when her father called from downstairs.

"Melanie! Hey, Mel, I made bacon and eggs."

"What?" she muttered, with an irritated glance at the clock. The time was barely four-thirty, and her father—who never cooked—was serving breakfast for dinner. He had to be halfway crocked.

"Come on down!" he insisted. "I'm putting in the toast."

"Coming," she called back, reluctantly shoving the diary under her pillows.

"I'll get back to you," she promised it.

But when? There was no telling how long her father would keep her downstairs, and she had a load of homework to do.

That's all right, she thought as she walked down the marble staircase and headed toward the kitchen. She'd been reading the diary in bits and pieces anyway, stretching it out, trying to make it last. When she was reading her mother's life, written in her own hand, Melanie felt a bond she hadn't known since her mother's death. She didn't want it to ever end, but she knew it would, the day the pages ran out. *If I don't get back to it today, then maybe tomorrow. Maybe not until Friday.*

As long as her curiosity lasted, her mother was alive. There was no need to rush through the story.

She already knew how it ended.

"No, I'm definitely coming this Saturday," Peter assured Chris Hobart over the phone. "I can't expect you and Maura to hold down the fort forever."

Peter and Chris, his college-age partner in the Junior Explorers program, normally spent every Saturday morning with the kids in Clearwater Crossing Park. Since Sarah had been in the hospital, though, Chris and his girlfriend, Maura Kennedy, had been covering for Peter so that he could be there for Jenna.

"We don't mind," said Chris. "Take as long as you need to."

"No, I *want* to come back. There's no telling how long Sarah will be in the hospital, but Jenna seems to be doing better. Besides, I miss the kids. I don't want them to think I've abandoned them."

"Nah, they understand. I told them about Sarah."

"Even so." Peter shifted his position in the overstuffed den chair. "Hey, have you given any more thought to having a day camp this summer?"

Chris sighed over the line. "I like the idea, Peter, but I don't see how I can do it. I always take a job in the summer, and this summer I was planning to take a couple of classes, too, to make sure I graduate on time. Between school and everything else, it's hard enough just to keep my Saturdays free."

"Oh," Peter said, too disappointed to hide it.

"I'm sorry. If you decide to go ahead without me, though, I'll still help as much as I can. Saturdays, fund-raisers, you name it."

Peter toyed with the telephone cord, feeding his finger through the loops. He had really wanted Chris on board for the day camp, but he should have realized it was impossible. Estranged from his family, Chris was putting himself through college by means of financial aid and whatever odd jobs he could get. "I guess . . . I guess we could do it without you," he said doubtfully, still trying to accept what he should have known all along.

"You guess? Of course you can!" Chris encouraged. "You're a lot older now than when we started the park program, plus you've earned everybody's trust. You don't need me anymore."

His voice dropped to a more sober tone. "Besides, quite honestly, I'm not sure how much longer I can be around anyway. There are a lot of things coming up. Junior year and . . . well, just a lot of things. This could be my last summer with the kids."

"What kind of things?" Peter demanded.

"Things, all right? Come on, Peter. I'm turning twenty-one next week. We knew when we started this couldn't last forever. People grow up. They move on."

"I honestly never thought about it."

"Well, you'd better start. Next year you'll be a senior, right? And unless you're planning to ditch College of the Ozarks for CU—"

"Jenna would kill me," Peter said quickly, not even wanting to think about it.

"See? That's all I'm saying. All good things must come to an end."

"Peter! Dinner!" Mrs. Altmann called from the kitchen.

"I have to go. I'll see you Saturday."

His parents were already seated when Peter pulled up his usual chair at the table.

"Everything looks great, Mom," he said automatically, glancing listlessly at the food.

"Is something the matter?" she asked. "Who were you talking to?"

"Just Chris. He said this could be his last summer with the Junior Explorers. And I just realized that next summer could be mine. How depressing."

"Is that all?" His father's smile was a little sad. "Time goes by whether we want it to or not. Come on, let's say grace."

But as soon as the plates were loaded with corned beef and cabbage, Peter's thoughts went back to the Junior Explorers.

"Chris won't be able to help me if I do the day camp, either. I might get some help from Eight Prime, but I doubt that any of them will commit for a whole summer."

"They wouldn't need to, would they?" asked his mother. "If you could get three or four weeks from each of them, you could stagger the time to cover three months."

Peter cut a bite of potato and chewed it thoughtfully. "Jenna would probably help all summer. I suppose it could still be done, if we could figure out a place to do it. I've been racking my brain, but so far I've got nothing."

"You could always keep your base at the park. The kids are used to going there."

"They're too used to it. That's the problem. Camp is supposed to be new, and different, and exciting."

His father reached for the butter. "Have you asked the kids how they feel about the park? They might think a summer-long camp is pretty exciting no matter where you have it."

"No. I don't want to spill any beans until I'm sure this is going to happen. It would be awful to get their hopes up for nothing."

"That's smart," said his mother, nodding. "There's nothing worse than disappointing a kid. The way they look at you . . ." She shuddered.

"What about that old Boy Scout camp up on the

165

lake?" Mr. Altmann asked suddenly. "It isn't much, but it might be all right if you did a little fixing."

"Aren't the Boy Scouts using it?" Peter asked dubiously, not sure where his father meant.

"Not anymore. They moved around to the other side of the lake way back in . . ." Mr. Altmann scrunched up his face, trying to remember. "Well, before you and David were born, anyway. The last time I was there, though, the old buildings were still standing. They had a little dock, too, if I remember right. That might be gone now."

"We could live without a dock." Peter sat up straighter in his chair. "Did they have any ball fields?"

"I'd totally forgotten that old place existed," his mother interrupted dreamily. "Your father and I used to go up there when we were just teenagers. You know, to see the lake."

"Yeah, I know why teenagers go to the lake," Peter teased.

"Peter!" she exclaimed.

But Mr. Altmann chuckled. "Those were the days, all right. You know, there are a couple of Scout leaders in the congregation, Peter. You might want to drive up and check the place out. If you think it'll work, you could ask how to get permission to use it."

"I'll do that," Peter said starting to get excited. "I'll go tomorrow." A trip to evaluate a potential campsite wouldn't count as unnecessary driving, and he'd be crazy not to follow up on a lead as good as this.

I wonder if Jenna would want to go with me?

The trip would be more fun with her along, but he was pretty sure she wouldn't want to miss an afternoon at the hospital. In fact, it might be insensitive of him even to ask, with Sarah so critical. *And what if it turns out to be a wild goose chase?*

Reluctantly, he decided not to mention his plan.

I'll just drive out there and check things out myself. If it looks good, I can always tell her later. After Sarah gets better.

Because Sarah *was* going to get better.

Wasn't she?

Peter closed his eyes. *Dear God, please let her live.*

"Knock it off, Leah," Miguel whispered nervously, his eyes darting toward her half-open bedroom door. "What if your mother comes in here?"

"What if she does?" Leah teased, not taking her hands off his shoulders. He was sitting in the chair at her desk, leaning over a book while she leaned over him. "This is so tame I'm afraid she'll be disappointed. But maybe if I tickled you . . ."

Giggling, she dropped her hands to his ribs. She had barely made contact, though, before he spun the chair around, grabbing both her wrists.

"Will you knock it off? I don't need your parents

thinking I'm a pervert the first time I'm allowed in your room."

Leah laughed, unconcerned. "No. We'll save that for the second time."

"I'm warning you, Leah. Keep it up, and I'll go study out in the living room. You're making me look bad."

"Don't be such a worrywart! I'll tell you what: If either of my parents comes in here, I'll tell them *I* was taking advantage of *you*."

"*That* makes me look better," he grumbled. "Now I'm not even a man."

"Oh, all right. Have it your way," she relented, twisting her wrists free. Her parents trusted her completely, or Miguel wouldn't be in her room in the first place, but there was no point making him so uncomfortable he refused to ever come back. "What are you reading?"

"History. I thought you had a bunch of math problems."

"I do." But sitting on her bed wading through precalculus homework hadn't been nearly as interesting as watching the nape of his neck and imagining covering it with kisses.

"So?"

"It's just such a rare event that I get you away from Sabrina that I want to make sure I enjoy it to the fullest."

Miguel winced with annoyance. "It will be fine with me anytime you want to get off Sabrina's case. She doesn't even usually make the schedule—her dad does. And when she does, and she puts me on it, so what? That's my job."

Leah knew she should keep her mouth shut, but she felt like she'd held back so long that she'd explode if she didn't say *something*. "Look, Miguel, I know *you* only think of Sabrina as a friend, but—"

"That's right. We're friends," he said emphatically. "Why wouldn't we be? I've known her practically all my life. Besides, everyone likes Sabrina, and so would you, if you knew her. She's really smart, really funny, and really good at what she does."

"Not to mention really pretty."

"What?"

"Don't you think she's pretty?"

"Of course. But once again, so what? Who cares?"

"I care," Leah said, mentally chalking another black mark by Sabrina's name. Then the rest came spilling out. "I don't know why, but I can't help feeling like she's trying to come between us. It's like she's just waiting for me to leave, and the moment I do, she'll be right there, trying to take you away."

"That's ridiculous! What makes you think that?"

"I can't explain," she admitted. "It's just a hunch. But from the very first day I saw her, the way she was looking at you . . ."

"You're crazy," Miguel said flatly.

"I don't think so, Miguel. Maybe you didn't see it, but—"

"I didn't see it, because there was nothing to see," he told her, laughing with disbelief. "You imagined the whole thing."

"I hope so," Leah said sulkily.

"You did." Taking her chin in one hand, he trained her eyes on his. "I can assure you that Sabrina is not the least bit interested in me. All right?"

She didn't answer.

"All right?" he repeated loudly.

She nodded, but it wasn't. Not in the least.

Sabrina wasn't interested in him? What was that supposed to mean? That *he* was interested in *Sabrina*?

Thirteen

"It's for you," Heather said disgustedly, sticking her head into Nicole's room on Thursday night just long enough to fling the cordless phone into her pillows. "Some guy."

"A guy?" Courtney snapped to attention at the foot of Nicole's bed. "Do you think it's *the* Guy?"

Nicole was already diving to find out. "Hello?" she said breathlessly, fumbling the phone to her ear while trying to clear a seat a safe talking distance from Courtney. "This is Nicole."

"You sound like you've been running," Guy said with a chuckle. "Did I catch you at a bad time?"

"No. No I was just doing some, um . . . research," she said, not wanting to reveal that she and Courtney had been comparing makeup tips in the magazines she was now pushing out of the way. "What are you doing?"

"Not much. Homework. My school gives out a ton. Does yours?"

Nicole glanced uneasily at the untouched stack of

books on her desk. "Uh, some. It varies." How much of it she did varied, anyway.

"How is Sarah?"

"About the same, I think. But Jenna's doing better. She seemed almost normal at school today."

Courtney rolled her eyes, telegraphing the unlikelihood of Jenna's ever being normal as far as she was concerned.

Nicole averted her gaze. "I'll probably go by the hospital again this weekend," she added quickly.

"I was calling about this weekend. I thought maybe, if you weren't too busy, we could catch a movie or something."

Yes! she wanted to shout. Instead she took a deep breath and managed to sound offhand. "A movie would be fun. I could go on Saturday night."

"All right. I'll pick you up at seven. That way we'll have some time beforehand to choose one at the theater."

"Sounds good. I'll see you then."

Nicole hung up the phone, thrilled with the way she had handled things. For once she had sounded interested but not *too* interested. Willing but not desperate. By suggesting they go on Saturday night, she had even managed to imply that she might not be free the entire forty-eight hours of the weekend, which made her practically a genius.

Then Courtney jumped into her act.

"A date on Saturday? Excellent!" she said, leaning

forward to point toward the phone. "Now call him back and say you want to double with me and Jeff."

"What? No!"

"What do you mean, no? I thought you were my best friend."

"I am, but . . ." She couldn't even imagine doing something so embarrassing.

"It doesn't have to be a big deal," said Courtney, reading her mind. "You just have to do it right. Be casual, the way you just were."

"You thought I was casual?" Nicole puffed up at the rare flattery from her friend. "I thought I did pretty good too."

"All you need is a line. I know!" Courtney smiled broadly, her eyes glittering. "Call and tell him you want a do-over of that first blind date with me and Jeff, the one that went so badly. Like you guys are starting over from scratch, you know? Say you want to erase the past."

"I don't know," Nicole said reluctantly.

"Come on, Nicole! All Jeff needs is a push. If you tell Guy we should all go out, then he'll tell Jeff that I'm going to say yes. Don't you see? No more waiting."

"If you want him pushed so badly, why don't you call Jeff yourself?"

"Are you crazy? I have my pride. He broke up with me, don't forget. He has to make the first move."

"Can't he make it on his own?" Nicole pleaded.

But Courtney was insistent, revising and refining what she wanted Nicole to say until it sounded almost reasonable. "Come on! Guy will be flattered. Who wouldn't?" she concluded, pointing to the phone again. "Call now, before too much time goes by."

Nicole was fairly composed as she dialed Guy's number, but by the time he finally answered she was wishing she'd never called.

"Hi. It's me. Again," she said nervously. "Long time, no talk."

Courtney grimaced and held her nose, which wasn't exactly calming. Nicole's hand grew slick on the plastic receiver. Her stomach turned a few flips.

"Hi, Nicole. What's up?"

She froze, unable even to speak. Courtney released her nostrils and made frantic "go ahead" motions.

"Nicole?"

"I was just wondering. I mean, I was thinking," she blurted out like a total fool. "Wouldn't it be fun to double date again? Like we did the last time we went to the movies. I mean the first time. That is, I mean, you know . . . with Jeff."

"You want to invite Jeff?" He sounded less than thrilled by the prospect.

"Well, yeah. But only because it would be like the first time we went out, remember? I thought maybe we could do that again."

"Why? I didn't think anyone enjoyed it that much the first time."

She was saying everything wrong. Courtney pantomimed frantic choking motions, her tongue lolling out and her green eyes popping.

"No, um, that's the whole point. It was really kind of awful. But I thought if we did it over—did it *right*, I mean—we could kind of erase the other time. Like it never happened. Like everything went smoothly between us right from the very start."

She hadn't put it nearly as well as Courtney had, but at least her friend took her hands from her throat, staring intently while they waited for Guy's reaction.

"I, uh, I guess I'm just kind of surprised. I didn't think you and Jeff were even speaking to each other."

"It's not that we're not *speaking*. It's just that we haven't been, you know, talking that much lately."

"There's a difference?"

"Look, if you don't want to, it's no big deal." She squeezed her eyes shut to block out Courtney's hysterics. "It was just a spur-of-the-moment idea. I thought it might be fun."

"It might be," Guy allowed. "If that's what you really want to do."

"Totally up to you," she squeaked, trying to catch her breath.

"Well, maybe I'll give Jeff a call. But I don't know if he'll be free."

"Whatever. Either way. I'll just see you Saturday night, all right?"

She was nearly hyperventilating by the time she hung up the phone. "I can't believe you made me do that!" she wailed at Courtney. "What a disaster!"

"I'll say! You never even mentioned my name! You were supposed to say you wanted to double with Jeff and Courtney. Jeff and *Courtney*, remember?"

Had she really never mentioned Courtney? Nicole's hands were shaking, and she was still so agitated she could barely remember half the conversation.

"Well, I'm not Jeff," she defended herself. "I can't invite you out *for* him. Besides, it was obvious enough. I'm sure Guy knew what I meant."

Courtney stopped to think. "He'd be an idiot not to," she admitted at last.

Nicole relaxed a fraction.

"In fact, maybe you played it just right. We don't want Jeff thinking I'm desperate—*or* that I had anything to do with this. No, I think you finally got it right, Nicole. Understated, that's the way to go. All I have to do now is go home and wait for Jeff to call."

She rose from the bed, as if to put her plan into instant action.

"Yes, but it may not be *this* weekend," Nicole warned quickly. "Guy said he'd ask, but what if Jeff's already busy? It may have to be next weekend. Or the one after that. Besides, why run home and wait for the phone to ring? Let Jeff wonder who you're out with."

Courtney raised a finely plucked brow. "Devious," she said approvingly. "I like the way you're starting to think."

Dropping back onto the bed, she picked up a magazine. "So what should we do? Try some of these hairstyles, or sneak downstairs and eat the rest of your mom's pudding cake?"

Nicole took a few deep breaths, trying to return her heart rate to normal. "You really think I did all right?"

"I said it was good. What do you want? A medal?"

"I guess we can eat the rest of the pudding cake, then." She'd only had a spoonful at dinner, so one more might not kill her. "If that's what you really want to do."

"Who wouldn't? I could eat that stuff by the truckload." Courtney bounced to her feet with a smile on her face. "I can't wait to see Jeff at school tomorrow. This will be so great! You have to be *sure* to meet me for lunch. By the cafeteria doors, all right?"

Nicole opened her bedroom door and they began walking toward the landing. "What about Emily?"

Courtney waved an impatient hand. "She can find us, or she can eat with someone else. But if Jeff decides to come to my table, I really want you there. I want you there anyway, all right?"

"All right," Nicole agreed, smiling as she followed her friend down the stairs.

Phoning Guy had been a nightmare, but one that had clearly paid off. She had totally proved her friendship to Courtney—and in a way Emily never could have.

Just keep on doing what you're doing, she told herself smugly, *and you'll cut that intruder out of the loop in no time*.

Miguel could hear the telephone ringing as he came up his walk after school on Friday. By the time he opened the door it had stopped.

"Miguel? Is that you?" his mother called from the kitchen. "I thought you were going to work."

"I am," he yelled back from the living room. "I'm just dropping off some stuff."

Mrs. del Rios appeared in the doorway between the two rooms. "There's someone on the phone from Clearwater General," she said in a low, worried voice. "Why is the hospital calling you?"

"It is?" Shrugging quickly out of his backpack, Miguel bounded past her to the kitchen phone. "Hello?"

"Is this Miguel?" a man's voice asked.

"Yes."

"This is Dr. Wells, pediatric surgeon at Clearwater General. I have your application for the student internship program here and I'd like to discuss it, if you have a minute."

Miguel's mother scrutinized him from the doorway, listening to every word. Dr. Wells's timing couldn't have been worse.

"Uh-huh."

"It says here that your primary interest is the children's ward, but that you would be open to other assignments. Do you have any experience working with children?"

"Well, um, not a lot." Turning his back to his mother, he tried to keep his voice low. "But I've been working with a charity that benefits some kids called the Junior Explorers, so I've been hanging out with them. And I have a sister who's fifteen, if that counts for anything. I think I could handle it."

"How do you feel about taking orders from a lot of different people and doing some pretty menial things? The student intern is just about the lowest man on the totem pole—it's not a glory position."

Miguel looked down at the white paint under his fingernails. "I'm pretty used to that."

Dr. Wells laughed. "Most teenagers are, I suppose."

"I have a lot of work experience, though. Probably more than most high-school students. I think, well . . . I probably have more experience in general."

"Yes," the man said thoughtfully. "You do seem uniquely qualified. Your essay is outstanding, Dr. Gibbons wrote a glowing recommendation, and with your family history, I think you're a perfect candidate. When can you start?"

"What? Well—I—uh . . ."

Miguel knew he should be thrilled, but all he felt was panic. Too late, he realized he'd been hoping that he wouldn't get into the program, that someone else would make his decision for him. Now he would have to choose. "I, uh, I'll need to check with a couple of people. Can I call you back later?"

"Sure. I'll be on the floor until eight tonight, or leave a message with my voice mail."

Miguel jotted down the numbers.

"I'll look forward to meeting you," Dr. Wells added. "Welcome aboard, Miguel."

"Um, thanks." He felt like a traitor, accepting congratulations when he'd probably have to decline the job, but what else could he say? "I'll talk to you pretty soon."

His mother had moved in to hover at his elbow. "What's going on?" she demanded the moment he hung up the phone. "Is there something you're not telling me?"

"No. Well, yes. But it isn't anything bad."

He sank into a dinette chair and his mom took the one across the table.

"Are you sick?"

"What? No. Not at all."

"Then why is the hospital calling?" she asked fearfully. "If I find out you're hiding—"

"They want to offer me a job, that's all."

"A job?" She blinked a couple of times. "Doing what?"

"It's not even really a job," he said, sighing. "It pays, but not very much."

"I don't understand. What would you be doing?"

"It's an internship program for high-school students. Ones who think . . . ones who think they might want to be doctors."

His mother stared, stunned.

"I know. It's crazy for me to even consider it, with money as tight as it is. I just . . . I thought I'd apply, and now I got in, and . . ."

His eyes begged her to talk him out of it. "I'd have to quit with Mr. Ambrosi. And who knows how I'd pay for medical school? The whole idea is—"

"Wonderful," she interrupted. "Amazing! Oh, Miguel, I'm so proud!"

"You are?"

"I had no idea you wanted to be a doctor, *mi hijo*. Oh, if only your father could be here now . . ." She wiped at the tears spilling onto her cheeks. "I'm sorry, but I'm just so happy."

Moving to his side, she wrapped both arms around his shoulders. "Congratulations, *mi vida*! When do you start?"

"I guess . . . I guess I should take it, then?" he said doubtfully.

She drew back with an astonished look. "Of course you should take it! Take it right away."

"But what about the money?"

"Will you please, please, *please* let me worry about the money? I'm perfectly well now, Miguel. I can manage on my own."

"But . . ." His mind was still full of misgivings, but seeing his mother so proud and happy, he knew he had to go through with it. "I guess I'll take it, then. Everything will work out somehow."

The smile that bloomed on her face seemed to light the whole room. Straightening up, she wiped away the last traces of tears. "Of course it will! Will you tell Sabrina tonight?"

Miguel shook his muddled head. "Tell her what?"

"That you're quitting, of course."

"No. Not tonight," he said quickly, cringing at the thought. "It would probably be better if I told Mr. Ambrosi, anyway."

"Yes," she agreed. "But do it soon, okay? They need to replace you, and besides, I can't wait to tell the world that my son's going to be a doctor!"

"Is David coming home this weekend?" Jenna asked.

Caitlin shook her head. "He can't. He's got midterms."

"Well, maybe next weekend," Jenna said, resuming her absent stare into space.

They were sitting up extra late with Sarah that Friday night, giving their parents some time alone together. Chairs pulled into position at their sister's bedside, they had already been there for hours and had long since given up pretending to read, embroider, or do anything useful.

"I hope Mom and Dad are having a good dinner," Caitlin ventured. "And I hope they went somewhere nice."

"Mmm," Jenna said through a yawn. "I thought they'd be here by now."

Resting her head against the edge of Sarah's bed, Jenna reached out and squeezed a bony knee through the thin blanket. "How about it, Sarah? Are you ready to call it a night?"

The leg moved under her hand. For a moment Jenna froze, paralyzed by a hope she was afraid to acknowledge. What if she'd only imagined it? What if—

Sarah's knee moved again, as if to twitch off a fly.

"Caitlin!" Jenna cried, leaping to her feet. "She's moving! I felt her move!"

They both leaned over their sister, searching her face. Sarah's eyes were closed, but for the first time her lids fluttered slightly, as if, as if . . .

"Open them," Caitlin whispered. "Come on, Sarah, you can do it." She took Sarah's hand and squeezed. "We're right here, waiting for you."

The leg Jenna had touched moved again, a slight jerk.

"I'm going for the doctor. I'll be right back." Caitlin gave Sarah's hand one last squeeze, then ran out of the room.

"Sarah? Sarah, it's me," Jenna whispered, gripping her by the shoulder. "Wake up."

Sarah's eyes fluttered. Then stopped. Then opened.

"Jenna?" she croaked, blinking against the bright lights.

"Yes! Oh, Sarah." Tears poured down Jenna's cheeks as she tried to hug her sister through the tubes and monitor wires. "I can't believe you're awake."

"I . . . I've been here a long time."

"Yes. Too long. Caitlin's here. She just ran to get the doctor. And Mom and Dad will be here any minute."

Caitlin skidded back into the room, followed by the on-duty doctor and a nurse.

"She's awake! She's talking!" Jenna cried joyfully, stepping back to let them see for themselves. They all started to crowd around until Sarah spoke again.

"Wait, Jenna," she said weakly, her eyes already closing. "Your cross . . . don't forget . . . you said . . ."

"I—you—you *heard* that?" Jenna stammered, dumbfounded.

But Sarah's eyes had closed. Her whole body seemed to deflate.

"Oh *no*," Caitlin moaned, grabbing Jenna's hand. "She's not in a coma again?"

"No," the nurse said gently.

184

Jenna felt the floor lurch beneath her. It couldn't be. Sarah wasn't . . . Not after everything that had happened.

"Is she dead?" she blurted out.

"No!" the doctor said quickly, looking up from the bed. "She's sleeping, that's all. Everything looks good. Very good, in fact. I think she'll be awake again tomorrow."

"I can't believe she heard us," Jenna whispered to Caitlin. "All that time we thought nothing was getting through and . . ." Her throat closed with tears.

"She was closer than we thought," Caitlin finished, wiping away some tears of her own. They stood there a moment in silence.

"I'll tell you what, though," Caitlin said suddenly, a smile filling her wet face. "You'd better let her wear that cross."

Wordlessly Jenna reached back and unclasped her favorite gold chain. Creeping forward to the bed, she fastened it gently around Sarah's neck, raining tears onto the blanket as she centered the cross on her sister's chest.

"You can keep it," she whispered, kissing Sarah's cheek. "I hope you wear it a long, long time."

Fourteen

Dr. Malone made a steeple of his fingers and smiled at the assembled Conrad family, in the waiting room Saturday morning.

"Good news," he announced with obvious pleasure. "We're moving Sarah to another room today. Her condition is stable, and if all goes well, she'll be home in a week or two."

"Thank God," Caitlin breathed.

"Finally!" Maggie squealed. She and Allison held hands as they jumped up and down, unable to contain themselves.

Jenna gave them a warning look, but she felt like screaming loudest of all. Sarah was all right! She'd be coming home soon! Jenna wanted to laugh, cry, and dance wild circles around the room, all at the same time. Her heart was full to bursting with the joy of her good news. She had to let it out, had to share it with someone. . . .

"I have to tell Peter," she heard herself say. Sarah had come out of her coma so late the night before that no one in Eight Prime even knew about it yet, and Jenna could only imagine the expression on Peter's face. "He'll be at the park with the Junior Explorers. Please, Mom, can I borrow your car?"

"How are we supposed to get home?" Mrs. Conrad asked, with an embarrassed glance at Dr. Malone.

"You'll all fit in Dad's van. Or I'll come back. I'll just go and come right back. I promise."

"Oh, let her go," Jenna's father said. "We'll be here all morning anyway."

"There *are* a few things I need to discuss with you," the doctor told them.

"All right," said Mrs. Conrad. "The keys are in my purse."

"Thank you!" Jenna cried.

She hugged her mother, found the keys, then ran for the elevator. She was already driving out of the parking lot before she had the first twinge of a second thought. She *was* still pretty mad at Peter.

"No. I'm done being mad," she said aloud. "How could I be mad on a beautiful morning like this?"

The sun was rising above the clouds, her sister was going to be fine, and Jenna's heart was so light she felt like she could forgive anything. She could forgive herself for her own faults and failings. She could forgive the drunken student who had nearly killed her sister. She could even forgive her boyfriend for kissing someone else.

"This is Peter's lucky day," she declared, laughing as she headed toward the park. And suddenly she realized that she couldn't wait to see him. All through the days since the accident he had tried to comfort her, but she had pushed him away. Even when they'd been together, there had been a wall between them. Now she wanted it down. She imagined a rubble of stone at her feet and herself scrambling over it, rushing to Peter's arms.

Taking the back road into the park, she drove to the staff-only parking lot and put on the brakes beside the Junior Explorers' blue bus. Leaping out of the car, she turned left, toward the activity center, but shouting on her right made her turn again. She had expected the kids to be inside, keeping warm. To her surprise they were swarming over the playground equipment, enjoying the weak sunshine.

"Jenna!" Peter called, spotting her. He stood to wave from the top of the monkey-bar dome, nearly losing his balance.

"Hi! Hi, I see you!" she shouted, running toward him.

The grass was wet, the sand under the playground equipment more like mud, but Jenna didn't slow in the slightest as she raced forward with her news.

Peter had scrambled down by the time she arrived at the bars. "What's going on?" he asked. "I thought you'd be at the hospital."

"I was. I just left." She wanted to draw out the suspense, to make her good news last, but seeing how worried he looked, she found that she couldn't hold back.

"Sarah's awake!" she cried. "She's out of the coma and she's talking!"

Peter's eyes went nearly round. For a moment he simply stared. Then both hands shot into the air. "Woo-hoo!" he shouted, as if his team had just scored the winning goal. "Jenna, that's terrific!"

Scooping her up, he swung her around in a circle. "I am so, *so* happy," he said, speaking her thoughts exactly.

They smiled at each other as he set her back on her feet, their whole hearts on their faces. Some of the kids had begun to run over, intrigued by the commotion, but Peter didn't let go. His arms held her as tightly as his gaze.

"I never stopped believing. Not for a minute."

"I did," Jenna admitted. "It felt like I died, then came back to life."

He nodded. "I was worried about you. But everything's fine now." He hesitated, his eyes still locked on hers. "It is, isn't it?"

She felt the blush rise on her cheeks, but she didn't look away. "Yes."

Pulling her even closer, he bent his face toward hers.

He's going to kiss me! she realized. She tensed, taken by surprise, then quickly turned her head. His kiss grazed her ear and landed in her hair.

"Wh—why?" he asked, letting go with a hurt expression.

Jenna's heart was pounding. She was sure her cheeks must be crimson. "The, uh, the kids," she said, nodding toward the mob bearing down on them.

As if to prove her point, Jason and Daneesha broke out of the front of the pack and hurled themselves into Peter's legs. "Peter's got a girlfriend, Peter's got a girlfriend," they taunted in singsong voices, inspiring the rest of the kids to join in. They danced a rowdy circle around the couple, chanting as they went.

"Yeah, yeah. Big news," said Peter, laughing good-naturedly. "Don't you kids need to go bother Chris or something?"

"We'd rather bother you." Wrapping her little fingers possessively around his, Lisa gave Jenna a "hands-off" look.

"I need to go anyway," Jenna said quickly. "Everyone's still at the hospital, and I promised my mom I would only stay a few minutes. Mary Beth is coming home again this afternoon, so . . . I'll, uh, I'll see you in church tomorrow."

"All right," he said, clearly disappointed. Perhaps he wanted to say more, but she hurried away before he could, a mess of confused emotions.

She had been so eager to see Peter and tell him her good news. After all, he was the person she loved most in the world, outside of her family. But when his lips had moved toward hers, all she could think about was his kissing Melanie Andrews. Had his eyes held that same expression? Had he put his arms around her the same way?

You were going to forgive him! she reminded herself as she ran toward her mother's car. *It's over! Can't you forgive and forget?*

But her hand shook as she put the key in the ignition, and her reflection in the rearview mirror looked nearly as tragic as if that morning's good news had never happened.

Maybe she could forgive, but she didn't think she'd ever forget.

Melanie lay stomach-down on the pale green carpeting in her poolhouse, her head propped up by bent elbows and her mother's diary open in the shaft of sunlight coming through a sliding glass door. Determined to finish the book uninterrupted that Saturday, she had left a note for her sleeping father saying she'd be gone all morning. Then, with the diary stuffed under her parka, she had walked out the door, around the front perimeter of the Andrewses' large property, and in through the gate on the far side of the poolhouse, sneaking into the little building unobserved. As much as her father liked to hang out and drink in there, she didn't think he'd bother so long as he wasn't expecting her home. Why hide out when he had the main house to himself?

"And I only need a little longer now," Melanie muttered, leaning onto one elbow to turn the page.

As she had predicted, things weren't going well with Tristyn and Trent's elopement. Trent had promised to work out the details before the end of the week, but it was hard to do anything secret in such a small town, and every inquiry seemed to mean driving for hours, losing precious time. Worse, Tristyn and Trent both had shopping and packing to do, there were people to bid good-bye, end-of-summer parties to attend . . . and both sets of parents were becoming increasingly adamant about keeping their soon-to-be-college-bound teens home as many hours as possible. With every day that slipped by, Tristyn's anxiety grew, until, in the entry written two nights before they were supposed to leave for college, she was a nervous wreck—and Melanie suddenly discovered she had chewed a fingernail down to the skin. She snatched it out of her mouth as her eyes skimmed the next entry of large, agitated script.

> I can't believe this is happening. Now what am I supposed to do? If I'm going with Trent, I have to leave tomorrow, but Mom and Dad will kill me if I run off without getting married. I mean, they're not going to be too happy either way, but at least if I'm married people won't be able to say too much. Oh, they'll still talk—they always do—but Mom

will be able to hold her head up around those old biddies at church. Except that it's too late now, and I don't know what to do. Trent says we ought to just get married in Clearwater Crossing. It will be easy there because we're both eighteen and there won't be anything left to hide once we're gone. I know he's right—but I really wanted to be married first. It would have made everything so much better. Now we'll have to move in together before the wedding, because no way can we afford two places. If our parents cut off our college money, I'm not even sure how we'll afford one. I'll have to get a job right away—and that's fine—but I wish I knew what to do right now. Tonight.

I can't go with him. But how can I go to New York without him? And I certainly can't stay here. The smart thing might be to wait, but Trent doesn't want to and neither do I. Besides, why should I bother starting college when I know I'm not going to finish? I know what I want to do with my life now, and the only thing standing between me and happily-ever-after is a stupid piece of paper. That's all a marriage license really is, right? A piece of paper with a date on it? And when Trent and I are old, and rocking on the porch with ten grandchildren, is it really going to matter if the date says this week or next? No one will even remember, let alone care.

If I were smart, I'd just pack one suitcase with the stuff I really need and sneak out of town with Trent tonight. That's what he wants to do. He's taking his car to Missouri anyway, so we could just leave notes for our parents and go. Then, in a week or two, when we're married and have a place of our own, we could come back for the rest of our things. Maybe we'd even have a little reception or something. That would be the way to do it. If my parents didn't kill me. But I can't keep living my life by what my parents want me to do! I'm eighteen now, grown up, and I'm going to be married. Who should I listen to? Mommy and Daddy, or my future husband? If I don't leave with Trent now, what is he going to think? That I don't really love him? That I'm not serious about being his wife? This would all be a lot easier if he had just figured out how to get married this week, like he said he was going to. Or he could have proposed a little earlier. But I'm the one holding us back now. If I blow this, I'll hate myself for the rest of my life.

So I have to go. Wow, it's that simple. I ought to go right now, too, before it gets any later. I'm just going to drop this book off at Lisa's house, say good-bye, and then go home and pack. She can send it to me later, when Trent and I get settled.

This is so weird. I can't believe I'm actually

doing this! But I guess everyone has to grow up sometime.

Okay, then. This is it. Wish me luck!

Holding her breath, Melanie flipped the page, only to be confronted by blank paper. "That's not the end! Oh no! It *can't* end here!"

She had known she was close to the back cover—what she hadn't realized was that there was no writing on the last twenty or so pages of the book. She flipped frantically through them now, just to be sure. Nothing.

"No, Mom, don't leave me hanging!"

How would she ever find out what had happened?

Pushing to her feet, she paced up and down the poolhouse, the diary in her hands. She felt like she knew her mother better than ever now, but at the same time she had only half the story. Had her mother really left home that night? If so, what had happened? And if, by some inconceivable sequence of events, Tristyn *had* actually married Trent, how did Melanie and Mr. Andrews fit into the picture? Neither of them had even existed for Tristyn at the time she'd written the diary.

"I *have* to find out."

But how?

Did Aunt Gwen know? Would it do Melanie any good if she did? *When I asked her about Mom before, she said I should talk to my dad.* Melanie had ruled that out even before she knew there was another man involved, but *now* . . .

"No way," she said with a shudder. "What about Lisa Kelly?"

Tristyn had apparently never sent for the diary, and Lisa had thought enough of her friend to keep it all those years. Would Lisa know what had happened? If she did, would she tell Melanie?

Or maybe there was a better way. Could Melanie research the past on her own? If Tristyn and Trent had married in Clearwater Crossing, would she be able to find their marriage certificate downtown at City Hall? For that matter, would her parents' certificate be there too? A horrible new thought gripped her: Were her parents actually married?

"Ohhhh, I don't know, I don't know, I don't know," she groaned, pulling her hair in frustration.

She only knew that she had to find out.

Passing the bar at the end of the main room, she rushed down the short hall to the bathroom, yanked open a linen closet, and hid the diary under some towels. Then she hurried back to grab her coat and ran out into the cool late morning.

I just have to think. If I concentrate, I can figure this out.

But her mind was spinning a thousand different ways as she walked toward the creek on the back of her property. How could she think when she didn't know *what* to think?

"I hear a car," said Nicole, peering through her bedroom window into the darkness outside. "I'll call you tomorrow."

"All right," Courtney said reluctantly. "But find out why Jeff didn't call me. Was he busy this weekend or what?"

"I'll *try*," Nicole promised for at least the fifteenth time. But as she hung up the phone, she couldn't say she was sorry that the requested double date hadn't materialized. She had never really wanted to double anyway—that had been Courtney's idea—and now she could enjoy Guy's undivided attention with a clear conscience.

The doorbell rang. Nicole was already on her way downstairs. "I'll get it!" she yelled, determined to keep Heather from Guy at all costs. They already knew each other, but there was still no telling what kind of damage the little creep could do. On their last date, Nicole had managed to whisk Guy away so quickly that none of her family had even seen him. "Mom, I'm leaving!" she called from the stairs, hoping to repeat a miracle.

But both of her parents were already at the front door. "We want to meet your young man," said her mother, looking way too eager. Her father nodded, a newspaper dangling from his hand.

"Oh, great," groaned Nicole. "Listen, just *please* don't call him that." She opened the door right as Heather ran up to join the gawk-fest.

Guy was standing in a puddle of light on her doorstep, looking like a pillar of sanity compared to the people behind her.

"Hi, Guy," Nicole said shyly.

"Hi, Guy," Heather mocked behind her.

Nicole closed her eyes and willed her sister to another planet.

"You look nice," Guy said, encouraging her to open them again.

"Really? Thanks." She tried to act as though she were used to getting compliments, but she'd been changing her clothes, hair, and makeup for the past three hours, hoping for something like that. "I mean, uh, so do you."

Her mother cleared her throat. Reluctantly Nicole opened the door a little wider.

"My parents want to meet you. This is my mother, and my father. You know Heather. And this is Guy. All right? Well, I guess we're on our way!"

"Where are you kids going?" Mr. Brewster asked Guy.

Nicole grimaced, mortified. He already knew, for one thing, and did he have to call them kids?

"To the mall for a movie," Guy answered respectfully. "But I don't know what we're seeing yet. There are a couple different choices."

198

"I heard that the new Disney movie is just *adorable*," Mrs. Brewster said.

Heather snickered and Nicole knew exactly where her mom had heard that.

"Yes, well, we'll pick one when we get there," she said quickly. "And we might go somewhere afterward, so don't wait up."

"I expect you home by midnight. Not a minute later."

"Mommmmm!" she wailed.

"Don't worry," Guy said. "I have to be home by midnight too, so you'll be home way before curfew."

"Oh good," she said sarcastically, wondering why everyone was smiling.

Finally she got him out onto the stoop and closed the door behind them. "I'm so sorry to have put you through that. You probably would have had to meet them eventually, though, so at least it's over with."

"Does that mean you're planning on keeping me around?" Guy was wearing an old dark blue sweater beneath a bulky down parka. His jeans were faded, his shoes nondescript. But there was something about the way his hair spilled over his smiling eyes that made her forget about clothes.

"Do you want me to?" she countered, suddenly very nervous.

Guy laughed. "Come on," he said, directing her to his car. "I have a surprise for you."

"A surprise?" she repeated. "What is it?"

But when Guy opened her passenger door, triggering the light inside his car, she thought she was going to pass out.

"Hi, Nicole," said Jeff Nguyen from the backseat.

And beside him a redhead Nicole had never seen before smiled like a game-show winner, one pale hand entwined with his.

"Hi. I'm Hope," she said. "Nice to meet you."

"Oh my . . ." Nicole held the edge of the door for support. "My . . ."

The girl looked like Courtney after a year of reform school and a 1950s makeover. *She . . . she's the Anticourtney!*

"You said you wanted to double with Jeff," Guy reminded her happily, handing her into her seat. "Surprise!"

You can say that again, thought Nicole, managing a weak smile.

"Jeff and Hope have been dating awhile, but I didn't know if they were ready to go public yet," Guy said, climbing in on the driver's side. "I went ahead and asked them, though, and here we all are."

"Here we are!" Nicole heard herself echo inanely.

Guy started the car, obviously pleased with himself.

Nicole had never been more horrified.

Courtney is going to kill me! she thought as Guy backed out of her driveway. *How could he not have known I meant we should double with Jeff and Court-*

ney? She's going to blame me for all of this. And then a new thought opened her eyes to the limit. *I told her that Jeff was still single!*

"So what does everyone want to see?" Guy asked. "Nicole's mom recommended the new Disney."

"Oh, I've been dying to see that!" Hope cooed. "But I was afraid you'd all laugh at me."

"Why would we laugh?" Jeff asked, sounding positively smitten. "If that's what you want to see, then I want to see it too."

Nicole closed her eyes. *Maybe I don't need to tell Courtney anything about this. It would be better if I don't. She'd probably prefer it if I don't.*

But how could she let Courtney keep pining over Jeff now? Not to mention that she was sure to ask when Jeff was going to call.

Well, I know the answer now, Nicole thought miserably. *Never.*

Fifteen

The final strains of the last hymn played as Jenna filed out with the rest of the choir. She had sung at both services that morning, lifting her voice high while her mother directed the singing, a beatific smile on her face.

"I'm so happy about your sister," Patty Johanssen told Jenna as they hung up their robes in the practice room. "Our whole family was praying for her."

"Thanks," said Jenna gratefully. Reverend Thompson had announced the good news before both sermons, and probably twenty other people had already said the same thing, but she didn't think she'd ever grow tired of hearing it. "I'll tell Sarah."

"Are you going out to the hall now?" Patty asked. "Do you want me to wait for you?"

The women's auxiliary had prepared a buffet of home-baked pastries and coffee that morning to celebrate the Conrads' good news. Everyone had been invited to stop by Fellowship Hall.

"Thanks, but you go on ahead," said Jenna. "There's just one quick thing I want to do first."

Patty smiled. "Okay. See you there."

Jenna fussed around straightening the robes, waiting until the room had emptied. Then she walked back down the hall to the sanctuary.

As she had hoped, the church had cleared out. Not a single person disturbed the sunbeams slanting through the stained-glass windows. Taking a seat in the first pew, Jenna bent her head to pray.

I just want to thank you again for watching over Sarah. And me. I can't believe how blessed our family is to still be together. I don't think I'll ever take that for granted again. Well . . . you might have to remind me, but it will take something a lot less spectacular next time. I wish I could show you how grateful I am. I've decided that the best way is just to be the very best sister I can. When things don't go so great at home, and maybe I get a little annoyed, I hope I'll remember this promise and how truly lucky I am to have a family healthy enough to bug me.

Unbowing her head, she rose halfway to her feet before a last-minute thought dropped her back into the pew.

And God? Could you please help me figure out what to do about Peter? I know I haven't been treating him right, and I know he cares about me. I care about him too. So much. But every time I think about him with Melanie . . .

She shivered and stood up, glad to be talking to someone who didn't need her to finish the sentence.

* * *

Peter ran excitedly across the hospital parking lot, in a hurry to find Jenna and tell her what he'd just learned. *You better slow down*, he thought, reluctantly reining in to a trot, *or you're going to be all sweaty when you get there*.

Taking the elevator up to Sarah's new floor, he walked down the hall looking for the room number Mr. Conrad had given him between services that morning. Peter had been sorry to miss the celebration after the second service, but after the first one his father had introduced him to Mr. Wylie, one of the Scout leaders, and there had been such exciting developments that Peter had decided to go directly out to the lake and catch up with Jenna at the hospital later.

He had already been to the lake once that week, to check on the old Scout camp. The location was perfect for little kids, just a quarter-mile hike from the main parking lot, with lots of big trees for shade. But the facilities! The skeletal remains of a short dock rotted in the mud, while a couple of long split logs apparently served for seating. The only building left on the site was a remarkably ramshackle old shed, weathered gray, with all its windows broken. And that was everything. No playing fields, no boathouse, no changing rooms, no bathrooms. *Heck, no running water*, he'd thought, discouraged.

As badly as Peter had wanted it to work, he

couldn't imagine proposing the site to Eight Prime. The girls would be sure to scream about the lack of bathrooms, and while there were toilets back at the parking lot, the kids were too young to send off by themselves. Even he couldn't imagine making a half-mile round trip every time one of them needed to go. Maybe Eight Prime could fix up the shed and the dock, but that would take a lot of time and money. And if they had to pay to use the camp too . . .

His father had convinced him to talk to Mr. Wylie anyway. And was he ever glad he had! The smile on his face almost hurt now, the way it stretched from ear to ear.

A door to a room stood open ahead, a couple of familiar-looking backs visible in the doorway. Peter hurried the final distance.

"Hi!" he said, greeting Mary Beth as enthusiastically as if he hadn't just seen her in church that morning. "Is everybody here?"

"Can't you tell?" she asked with a sardonic smile.

Sarah's new room was smaller than her previous one. Her seven family members packed it to capacity. Peter craned his neck and caught just a glimpse of her blond head, well propped up with pillows, between the people lining her bedside.

"Shove on in," said Caitlin. "Maybe Maggie will give you an inch."

"Are you sure it's all right?" he asked, bursting to do just that but not wanting to be rude.

Mary Beth chuckled, a mixture of happiness and relief. "Don't worry. Sarah is *loving* all this attention."

Peter held his breath and edged in sideways next to Jenna. "Hey, Sarah!" he said, smiling to see her eyes open. "Don't you know you're supposed to use a stunt double for the really scary stuff?"

"Oh, Peter," she said, giggling. A nasal oxygen tube divided her face. Her voice was raspy, her giggle weak, but it was such a thrill just to have her respond.

"I brought you something." Digging into his pocket, he removed a small gift he'd bought the first weekend after she'd been hurt. "I've been waiting to give you this."

Her mother helped her remove the wrinkled tissue. "An angel pin! How cute," Mrs. Conrad said.

Sarah smiled, pleased. Then a worried expression came over her face. "That reminds me," she murmured, staring at the pin as if trying to recall. "I had the weirdest dream. I saw an angel in my room, bending over my bed. She touched my head, like this."

Peter felt the hair rise on the back of his neck as Sarah drew a hand across her forehead. He had heard that story before, from a completely different person.

But Mrs. Conrad simply smiled and fastened the pin to Sarah's pajamas. "I don't doubt for a minute that there was an angel in your room. A hundred angels, for all we know."

Sarah nodded happily, admiring the way the tiny crystals sparkled on her lapel. A gold cross that looked just like Jenna's hung from her slender neck. Peter watched her a moment, then turned eagerly to his girlfriend.

"Can I talk to you out in the hall? I've got something important I can't wait to tell you."

Jenna tore her gaze from her sister. "All right. For a minute."

They traded positions with Allison and Mr. Conrad, then scooted past Caitlin and Mary Beth to get through the doorway.

"I got a great lead on a camp for the Junior Explorers!" Peter said the instant they were alone. His smile was actually starting to ache as he waited for her reaction.

"What?"

"I found a place that's going to work! At first I wasn't so sure, but I talked to Mr. Wylie between services today, and now I'm really excited."

She smiled faintly, not looking too convinced.

"No, wait until you hear," he said quickly. "It's a real pretty place on the lake, not *too* far from the parking lot. It needs some work—all right, a lot of work—but Mr. Wylie thinks we can get it for some token amount, like maybe a dollar a day. The place belongs to the park service, and if we donate the supplies and labor to fix it up, they might even let us use it for free."

Jenna still didn't look nearly as impressed as he'd thought she would. What had he left out?

"And there's water! I didn't think there was at first, but there's piping out to the camp from some old buildings they tore down. All we'd have to do is stub it out and put in a spigot. So there's our drinking fountain, and water for crafts and—"

"Are there bathrooms?" she asked.

He flinched at the direct hit to the weakest part of his plan. "Not exactly. There's a real nice bathroom at the parking lot, but if we want toilets at the camp, Mr. Wylie said we'd have to rent portable outhouses. You know the big blue kind?"

Jenna made a face. She knew.

"Okay, so that part's so not great," he admitted. "But once we fix the place up, we'll have a dock and a shed to store all our stuff in. Maybe we can even build some picnic tables. The kids can swim and fish and explore and collect rocks and do all kinds of things. It'll be a blast!"

"Ball fields?" Jenna asked.

"We'll have to use the park for that, but that won't be so bad. Maybe we'll hang out there a couple of mornings a week, then come out to our camp to swim in the afternoons."

"Lifeguards?"

Peter's smile died on his face. Was it his imagination, or was she going out of her way to pick holes in his new plan? He had expected her to be as happy as he was, but instead she seemed to be searching for every flaw.

"I think you just need to see it," he said slowly. "I'll grant you I don't have all the details worked out, but if Eight Prime agrees to this campsite, I'm sure we can make it suit us. I'm going to call the park service on Monday, and I think we ought to have an Eight Prime meeting next week. We need to plan the St. Patrick's Day sale, and probably a few more events besides."

"Okay. I need to get back to Sarah now." Jenna glanced over her shoulder at the doorway. "I'll see you at school tomorrow, all right?"

He could barely believe his ears. "Well . . . uh . . . sure," he said, stunned to be brushed off when he had just spilled such big news.

Jenna didn't even look back as she turned to rejoin her family, pressing into the crowded room.

What was that? he wondered, deeply hurt by her strange behavior. He hesitated a moment; then, not knowing what else to do, he trudged down the hall toward the elevators. *I really thought she'd be thrilled.*

Maybe he hadn't described it right. He punched the Down button and stepped inside, wondering if the problem was something he'd said.

I did make it sound like a lot of work. And a lot of

fund-raising. He shook his head, baffled. *But it will be a lot of work. That's never bothered her before.*

On the other hand, he'd never hit her with one of his big projects right after her sister had come out of a coma before, either.

That's it, he realized, slapping his forehead. *What an insensitive jerk I am! Of course she doesn't want to think about fund-raising right now.*

The Conrads had barely learned that Sarah was going to live, they were trying to have a private, family moment, and he'd just barged in like Mr. Clueless, expecting to monopolize Jenna's attention. He felt like an idiot. Even more of an idiot than the day before, when he'd tried to kiss her in front of the kids.

I'm sure she really is happy about the camp. Or she will be when she has a chance to think about it. In a few days, when Sarah is safely at home, everything can go back to normal.

Reasonably reassured, he walked out to his Toyota, wondering if he should go ahead and call the Eight Prime meeting. It couldn't hurt, but he wouldn't have minded having another, slightly more enthusiastic opinion about the Scout camp first, either—someone to back him up in front of the others.

I wonder what Melanie's doing right now? he thought suddenly. Melanie always had good ideas.

Maybe I'll just drive by and see if she wants to swing out to the lake.

* * *

"Miguel! What are you doing here?" Sabrina asked, opening the Ambrosis' front door wider.

"Are you eating dinner?" Miguel asked nervously. "Am I interrupting anything?"

"Not at all. Come in."

He hesitated a moment longer, until she pulled him in by his sleeve. "Everyone's going to be so surprised to see you," she said, beaming. "Come on. They're all down in the basement."

He followed her uneasily, still trying to figure out exactly what to say. "Your father too?"

She smiled back over her shoulder at him. "Of course."

She really is pretty, he thought distractedly, walking along behind her. It wasn't hard to see what made Leah so nervous. But the thought of him and Sabrina together . . .

Is a totally moot point, because after tonight I'll probably only ever see her at mass. That ought to be safe enough even for Leah.

He reached the basement stairs, irritated that the subject of him and Sabrina as a potential couple had ever come up. If *he* wasn't thinking about it, and *Sabrina* wasn't thinking about it, why did Leah have to put it into his head? Talking to Mr. Ambrosi was stressful enough without having to feel weird about that, too.

"Miguel!" Mr. and Mrs. Ambrosi greeted him

simultaneously. Two or three of the little Ambrosis waved from the couch in front of the television, while their slightly older siblings waged a heated Ping-Pong battle at the far end of the long room.

"You're just in time for dessert," said Mrs. Ambrosi. "We were about to have some cake upstairs."

"Thanks, but I can't stay," he said. "I was just hoping to speak to you, Mr. Ambrosi, if you have a minute."

His employer heaved himself out of his easy chair and ran a hand over his grizzled crewcut. "That sounds ominous. Is something the matter at work? Sabrina driving you crazy?"

"Daddy!" she protested, despite the fact that it was obviously a joke. "I'm not, am I?" she asked Miguel with a worried expression.

"Nothing like that," Miguel said quickly. "Except, well . . . it is about work. The thing is, something's come up and I have to quit. I'm really sorry."

"You're quitting?" cried Sabrina. "You can't quit! I *need* you."

"I can see why you decided to tell me and not my daughter," Mr. Ambrosi said dryly, with a sideways glance at Sabrina. "If you don't mind my asking, Miguel, what's come up?"

"I have a chance to be in an internship program at the hospital. I started out just wanting to volunteer there, but I was already so busy with school and work and everything. And then I found out I could get paid for being an intern if I got into this special program, so I decided to apply, but I didn't really think I'd get it, and then they called me and—"

"Congratulations." The smile on Mr. Ambrosi's face allowed Miguel to draw his first full breath since he'd entered the house. "If I were losing you to another construction company, I'd be pretty upset, but this sounds like a good learning experience for you."

"Thank you," Miguel said gratefully.

"I don't understand," Sabrina insisted. "Working for *us* is a good learning experience. How is working at the hospital going to teach you anything about being a contractor?"

"Oh. Well. There might be a change of plans," Miguel mumbled, embarrassed. "I'm thinking of being a doctor now."

"A doctor!" Mrs. Ambrosi exclaimed. "Are you serious, Miguel?"

He shrugged. "I'll find out, I guess. That's kind of what the internship is for."

"I think it's a fine idea," said Mr. Ambrosi, clapping him on the shoulder. "I hate to lose you, of course. But you're only, what—seventeen? It's too early to lock yourself into anything without exploring your other options."

"Thank you," Miguel said again.

"Maybe in the summer, if you have more time,

you'll want to come back to work for us. I don't know how many hours this internship thing is, but who knows? Maybe you'll be able to do both."

"I might," Miguel said eagerly. Why hadn't he thought of that? "If I can, I'd really like to."

"So we'll leave it loose, then. You can call me anytime."

Miguel pumped the big man's hand gratefully, then said good-bye to the family, declining a second offer of cake. He knew Mrs. Ambrosi made killer desserts, but he was supposed to take Leah out for ice cream. He hadn't even mentioned the internship to her yet, wanting to leave his options open until he had actually quit with Mr. Ambrosi, but now he planned to tell her the news over banana splits.

"I'll walk you out," said Sabrina, following him up the stairs. In the entry she hurried ahead of him, reaching for the knob. But instead of pulling the front door open she held it firmly closed.

"Are you sure this doesn't have anything to do with me?" she asked, facing him down. "I mean, if it does, I appreciate your not telling my father, but *I* really need to know."

"Sabrina! No," he assured her, refusing to consider how happy his change of employment was going to make Leah. Mollifying Leah wasn't the *reason* he was quitting, it was just a welcome bonus.

"That's a relief." She smiled a little, and then her smile turned sulky. "What am I supposed to do without you, Miguel? Did you even stop to think about how much I'd miss you?"

"Uh, honestly? No. I'm only part-time."

"Well, I will," she said, releasing the doorknob to step closer. "I thought we were getting along really well."

"We were," he said, not sure what to make of her behavior. The way she was looking at him . . . and she could hardly stand much closer if she tried. A sudden thought jolted his heart. Was she *flirting*?

"Now I don't know *where* I'm going to see you." She laid a hand on his arm, and this time Miguel understood why Leah had found that same gesture so threatening. There was a possessiveness to it, a hint of ownership he never should have missed.

"At church?" he suggested, trying to back up a little.

"Like that's going to do me any good! No, I want to see you alone. Just the two of us."

She can't possibly be suggesting what it sounds like, he reassured himself, sweat breaking out on his forehead. He swallowed hard a few times, then took the direct approach. "You, uh, you know I'm serious about Leah."

Sabrina smiled, her fingers pressing his flesh. "I know you're serious about her *now*."

Find out what happens next in Clearwater Crossing #13, *Dream On*.

About the Author

Laura Peyton Roberts is the author of numerous books for young readers, including all the titles in the Clearwater Crossing series. She holds degrees in both English and geology from San Diego State University. A native Californian, Laura Peyton Roberts lives in San Diego with her husband and two dogs.